Pride Publishing books by Ann Marie James

Everyone's Mechanic
Chasing the Dream
Fearing the Dream

I0542490

Everyone's Mechanic

FEARING THE DREAM

ANN MARIE JAMES

Fearing the Dream
ISBN # 978-1-83943-897-4
©Copyright Ann Marie James 2020
Cover Art by Erin Dameron-Hill ©Copyright June 2020
Interior text design by Claire Siemaszkiewicz
Pride Publishing

This is a work of fiction. All characters, places and events are from the author's imagination and should not be confused with fact. Any resemblance to persons, living or dead, events or places is purely coincidental.

All rights reserved. No part of this publication may be reproduced in any material form, whether by printing, photocopying, scanning or otherwise without the written permission of the publisher, Pride Publishing.

Applications should be addressed in the first instance, in writing, to Pride Publishing. Unauthorised or restricted acts in relation to this publication may result in civil proceedings and/or criminal prosecution.

The author and illustrator have asserted their respective rights under the Copyright Designs and Patents Acts 1988 (as amended) to be identified as the author of this book and illustrator of the artwork.

Published in 2020 by Pride Publishing, United Kingdom.

No part of this book may be reproduced, scanned, or distributed in any printed or electronic form without permission. Please do not participate in or encourage piracy of copyrighted materials in violation of the authors' rights. Purchase only authorised copies.

Pride Publishing is an imprint of Totally Entwined Group Limited.

If you purchased this book without a cover you should be aware that this book is stolen property. It was reported as "unsold and destroyed" to the publisher and neither the author nor the publisher has received any payment for this "stripped book".

FEARING
THE DREAM

Dedication

Thank you to my family for all of their support.

Chapter One

Stuart Woods slammed the door to his car and made his way to the open bay door of the garage owned by his friend Kirk. Everyone's Mechanic had become very popular, known for their quality work and high code of ethics. The Pride flag hanging outside the building was an indication that it was a safe place for all. Quality workmanship wasn't why he was here, though. This time Stuart needed to speak to his friend, Lee Clark.

"Hey, Lee," Stuart yelled through the open bay door and watched as Lee peeked his head out from under the hood of the bright orange Volkswagen bug he was working on.

"Stuart. What's up, man?" Lee made his way over, wiping his hands on a rag from his pocket as he walked.

"I heard a rumor that you got engaged last week. Why am I the last to know?" Stuart crossed his arms and arched an eyebrow in a way he hoped portrayed his upset over this fact, but he was worried that it probably came across as 'startled squirrel'. He had been practicing in the mirror. Lee's smirk didn't indicate that the practice had paid off, though.

"You told me two weeks ago that you had the website for some big landscaping company to design, so not to be offended if I didn't hear from you for the next few weeks. I didn't want to bother you when I knew you were busy," Lee said.

"You never bother me," Stuart countered. "I would have liked to have heard the news from you."

"I'm sorry. You're right. I should have called or stopped by, if for no other reason than to make sure you ate something." Lee pulled Stuart into a hug and patted his back. "How did you find out, anyway?"

"I ran into your fiancé's mama at the grocery store. She's very excited that you and Saul are engaged. I just wish I'd made my move on you sooner." Stuart laughed to show he was joking. It had stung for a while, but seeing Saul and Lee so perfect together showed him that they never would have worked. They did make kickass friends, though.

Lee chuckled. "Yeah. Man, excited isn't the word for it. Even though Saul and I have told her we just want something simple, she keeps calling with all these ideas for the wedding. As for the other... You were way too subtle for me, dude. I didn't even know you were hitting on me until Saul pointed it out."

"I wasn't one hundred percent sure you were gay. You're a big dude. I didn't want to get my ass kicked."

"Like you're that much smaller than me," Lee scoffed.

"I barely hit five-eleven and you outweigh me by probably fifty pounds."

"Whatever, dude." Both men broke into laughter.

"Seriously, Lee, I'm very happy for you. You guys are great together."

"Thanks. What about you?"

"What about me?"

"I saw you and Sergei talking at Kirk and Eric's wedding. Any news on that front?"

Stuart winced. "Nope. The guy got a phone call that he said was important and jetted without asking me for my number. I figured he wasn't really interested. I mean, why would he be? I found out who he really was after he left. The people around me were jealous that I even got to talk to him."

"Don't sell yourself short. It didn't look like he was disinterested to me."

Stuart shrugged. "It doesn't matter. He's out of my league anyway. I think the suit he was wearing cost more than my grocery budget for the year."

"Yeah, probably." Lee snort-laughed. "His loss."

"Thanks for saying so."

"It's the truth. I do have some weird news for you, though."

"Yeah? What's that?"

"A guy brought his bike in for service earlier this week."

"What's weird about that? You service a lot of motorcycles here."

"It was the motorcycle that I did the paintjob on for your brother's fortieth birthday."

"Really? You met my brother?" A big smile crossed Stuart's face. He had mentioned the name of the garage to his brother when he'd dropped his motorcycle back off with the new custom paint job he had paid for as his brother's birthday gift, but he didn't think the guy had actually been listening.

"Nope. I met the guy your brother sold his bike to."

The smile fell off Stuart's face. "What?"

"Your brother sold his bike pretty much the day after you gave it back to him, from what I could figure out. I thought you should know."

Stuart took a deep breath and released it slowly. "Thanks for telling me. I guess that's the last time I try to do something nice for him. I'm not sure why I even made the effort."

Stuart tried to shrug it off like it was no big deal, and he must have done a pretty effective acting job, because Lee looked like he'd bought it.

"Okay. As long as you're good with it."

"It was his gift to do with what he wanted. I'm not sure why he bugged me about mine, only to turn around and sell his once it was done, but whatever. I just wanted to stop by and tell you congratulations on your engagement, Lee. I'm very happy for you. Tell Saul I said congratulations too."

"Thanks. I will. Hey, I'm off Saturday and Saul has a safety class he has to teach at the sporting goods store. Do you have time to do lunch or something on Saturday?"

"Lunch would be great. The weather is supposed to be nice. How about we get the motorcycles out and head to Wilmington?"

"Sounds like an awesome idea. It's only a couple hours' drive from Raleigh. How about we leave around ten?"

"Sounds great. I'll meet you at your place at ten then."

"Oh, Saul is going to be so jealous," Lee said with a grin, clapping his hands together. "I can't wait. I've got to get back to this service ticket. See you Saturday."

With a final wave, Lee turned and headed back into the garage.

"See you." Stuart walked to his car, climbed in and fastened his seatbelt before starting it. He made sure to keep the smile plastered on his face, at least until he had turned out of the parking lot of the shop. He let the smile die once he was far enough away that none of his friends could see him. "That asshole!" Stuart yelled and slammed his hand down on the steering wheel. He didn't know why he was surprised that his brother had sold the motorcycle. He'd tried to do something nice for Andy since it was a big birthday — not that anyone in Stuart's family had given *him* a gift since he'd turned eighteen.

Stuart scoffed. "What family?" His father had died when he was six and his mother remarried when he was twelve. Stuart had been so excited. Not only would he get a dad, but he would get a brother too. Andy was ten years older and had seemed so cool to his preteen self. His stepfather had spent a lot of time with him prior to then and for about a year after the wedding.

Things had changed so slowly that Stuart hadn't really noticed at first, until family vacations had excluded him. And the day he'd graduated and a month after his eighteenth birthday, his stepfather Charles had told him he had to move out, since he was now out of high school. Stuart had been shocked. What had hurt the most, though, was that his mom had gone along with it. She'd just agreed with everything Charles had said, that *'a man needs to stand on his own two feet'*, which was ironic since Andy was living in the apartment above the garage, rent free. In fact, still today he lived in the apartment above the garage.

He had gone to Andy to ask if he could stay with him until he left for college. Andy had laughed at him and thrown him out. His mama had helped him pack his few belongings into the used car he had scrimped and saved for during his freshman and sophomore years of high school. He had worked any odd job he could find, as well as a job at McDonald's flipping burgers, as soon as he was old enough. Looking back, that should have been his first clue. Charles had bought his son a new car for his sixteenth birthday. Stuart was very thankful that he'd had the job when he'd gotten kicked out, though. His McDonald's job had allowed him to go to school with a scholarship.

He had also been lucky enough that his biological father's brother had let him live with him during breaks and holidays, as long as he contributed money toward groceries. He didn't know what he would have done without Uncle Peter. He was Stuart's only family, once he'd been cast aside. Unfortunately, the man had died the previous year of lung cancer caused by the pack-a-day smoking habit he had started as a teenager, leaving Stuart alone again.

Oh, his mother called once a month or so to check on him, but only when Charles wasn't home. Charles didn't want any other man in her life but him. Andy would also call him from time to time. In the beginning, it would be hidden with a request to hang out, which would morph into a request for money. During the last year or so, Andy hadn't even bothered with the hanging out part, though. He would call and ask for cash without any of the faking of brotherly affection. The last time Andy had stopped by to hit him up for some cash, his step-brother had seen Stuart's motorcycle with the custom paint job Lee had done on the gas tank. Andy had been so impressed with it that Stuart had offered to have something similar done on Andy's motorcycle for his upcoming fortieth birthday.

"Sucker!" Stuart yelled again as he pulled his car into the garage and shut the door. He walked into his kitchen and pulled a bottle of soda out of the refrigerator then stomped to his office. He should eat something, but he was too angry.

The hits had just kept coming that day. First, he'd been upset to find out Lee hadn't called to tell him about his vacation and engagement, then he'd received a phone call from his mom where she'd talked about the fantastic birthday party that Charles had thrown for Andy — which he, of course, wasn't invited to — then to find out the gift he had given him had been immediately sold.

"No more," Stuart promised himself. "Mom didn't even remember to wish me happy birthday today. She just rambled on about Andy's great party. I'm done. A lone wolf, that's me. From now on, I don't have or need family."

Stuart took a deep drink from his soda before looking around the office at the signs of his successful website design business. He pulled out his phone and blocked Andy's number. There was nothing left to say, after all. Sitting down at his desk, he got to work on his next project.

He remained focused on work until the ringing of the phone some unknown number of hours later startled him. Looking at the display, he saw the name and dorky picture of his college roommate Paul Williams on the screen. "Paulie! What's up?"

"Happy birthday!"

"You remembered."

"Of course I did, asshole. It's not every day that your best friend turns thirty."

"Uh-huh. Tell Chloe I said thanks for remembering." Chloe was Paul's kick-ass wife and a lawyer who never forgot anything, while Paul was an artist who worked for a giant mouse. They had moved to Florida for Chloe to go to law school and had never left.

"Yeah, yeah. Whatever."

Looking at the clock, he was shocked to see it was now close to dinner time. The hours had flown by while he had been in the zone. Standing up, he realized how stiff he had gotten. He twisted and stretched as he talked to Paul. After hanging up the phone a half hour later in a much better mood, Stuart was making his way to the kitchen to find something to eat when the doorbell rang. Looking out of the peephole, he was surprised to see Lee standing there. Opening the door, he was further surprised to see Saul, Kirk and his husband Eric, along with their girls Claire and Sam, all standing on his front porch.

He jumped when they all yelled 'Happy birthday' at him and started to sing the birthday song. Stuart felt himself tear up and had to look up at the roof of the porch to try to stop the flow.

"Aw, you guys remembered."

"Of course we did," Lee scoffed. "You didn't say anything earlier."

"Yeah, I flaked. Sorry about that." Lee pulled him into a hug and Stuart enjoyed the connection for a moment before letting go and moving down the line, hugging everyone.

"We brought dinner," Saul said, raising the bag of food in his left hand for Stuart to see. Glancing around, he saw everyone had at least one bag they were carrying.

"And cake!" Sam and Claire yelled together.

"Wow! Am I lucky or what?" Stuart answered the girls.

"Yep. Dad made you his famous pig pickin' cake. It's delicious," Claire answered.

"Thanks, Eric."

"We couldn't let this birthday go by without doing something. You only turn thirty once, after all."

"Thanks, everyone. Seriously, thank you."

"Unless you had other plans?" Kirk left the question dangling.

"Nope. My own mother didn't even remember to wish me a happy birthday when she called me earlier, so it's safe to say that I don't have any other plans."

"Ouch," Lee offered him a side-arm hug in sympathy. "Now I feel really bad about not remembering to say something earlier."

"All this more than makes up for it. Come on in. Let's get this party started." Stuart led the way through the door and turned left into the kitchen. After going to the cupboard, he pulled out plates and silverware for everyone and handed them to Saul to take to the table. "Is it okay if the girls sit at the breakfast bar? Sadly, my table's not quite big enough for everyone. I don't usually have anyone over to eat." Stuart shrugged as he finished the sentence.

Kirk chuckled. "Not a problem. Here, Saul." Kirk stuck out his hand to Saul. "Hand me two of the plates for the girls."

"We actually need one more plate," Lee said from where he was helping Saul set the table.

"Why? There should be one plate for everyone, unless I counted wrong."

Lee looked nervous and wasn't making eye contact. "Um, no. You didn't count wrong. There's one more person coming."

"What? Who?" Then suddenly it hit him who might be coming. "You didn't…"

Lee looked up briefly before quickly lowering his gaze to fuss with the silverware at the plate in front of him. "Um, maybe."

The peal of the doorbell interrupted them before Stuart could come up with a snarky reply. Kirk smirked at him over his shoulder. "I think that might be for you."

"It's my house, asshole. I should hope so." Stuart grumbled all the way to the door, before taking a deep breath to calm his nerves then opening it. He looked up into the gorgeous green eyes of Sergei Barinov. Hell, everything on the man was gorgeous, from his perfectly styled sable-brown hair, to his super-white teeth and his designer clothing. Today's ensemble included another suit that probably cost more than his mortgage payment.

After raising his gaze back to Sergei's eyes, Stuart winced when he saw the amusement staring back at him. "Sorry. Hi. Come on in." Stuart stepped back and waved Sergei into the house, closing the door behind him and directing him toward the kitchen. "Everyone is back here."

Sergei reached out and grabbed hold of Stuart's arm, stopping him in his tracks. "Before we join the others, I wish to first apologize for not getting your number at the wedding. It was a gross oversight on my part and one I want to correct before I leave here this evening."

Stuart had to swallow the saliva pooling in his mouth upon hearing Sergei's Russian-accented voice. Man, Sergei's voice did it for him. He shook his head to clear the lust-addled cobwebs from his mind.

"No? I cannot have your number?"

Stuart was quick to reassure him. "Yes, of course you can have my number. Was there something else before we join the others? You said 'first'?"

"Happy birthday, of course. I understand this is an important birthday for you?" As Sergei spoke, he leaned forward until he was almost whispering the words into Stuart's ear, making him shiver and swallow hard before he could answer.

"Yes. The big three-oh." Stuart forced himself to chuckle and step back, before continuing his trek to the kitchen. He shouted out as he walked down the hall. "Come on, everyone. Let the party begin. The final guest has arrived, so it's time to eat. What are we having?" Rubbing his hands together, he surveyed all the food laid out on the counters. "Holy cow, that's a lot."

Kirk laughed at him. "You have seen all of us eat, right? We'll have no problem eating this, and if there does happen to be anything left, I'm sure you'll enjoy the leftovers."

"That's true. Not having to cook for the next few days would be a definite positive."

"Lee says you guys are going to Wilmington for lunch Saturday on the bikes. I wish it wasn't my Saturday to work or I would have loved to go too. The weather is supposed to be perfect," Kirk said.

"Yeah. I'm quite excited." While Stuart had been talking, he had maneuvered himself away from Sergei, until he was standing on the other side of the counter from him. "Sergei, why don't you take off your suitcoat? We're not formal here. Oh, I guess we should have left the plates at the counter so everyone could get what they want."

Eric answered, "Yeah, we already thought of that. We moved the plates over by the refrigerator so everyone can just fill them then sit down."

"Great. Then let's get to eating. I'm starved."

"Didn't you eat lunch?" Claire questioned from by his elbow.

"Actually, no. I forgot." Stuart told the little white lie, looking away from Claire as he did so, only to be caught by Sergei's intense stare. Stuart found himself blushing a little, but no way was he telling Claire that he hadn't eaten because he was pissed off. "Come on, Claire. Let's see what we can find to eat."

After everyone had had their fill, Stuart was surprised to realize that there really weren't many leftovers. He pulled out some plastic containers, and Lee helped him store the rest of the food in the refrigerator. He wasn't really paying attention to what the others were doing, so he was completely startled when he closed the refrigerator and turned around to find everyone standing in front of him with a cake with two lit candles on top. He was thankful they had gone with a candle in the shape of the number three and another in the shape of the number zero and hadn't tried to cram thirty candles on the top of the cake.

He once again got a rendition of the birthday song. Claire and Sam threw in a couple of cha-cha-chas in this version. A shiver went down his spine as he heard Sergei's accented baritone. He couldn't stop his gaze from returning to the man, to find his surprise guest staring directly into his eyes. He had to force himself to look back at the candles on the cake. Once the song was complete, he leaned forward and blew out the candles to yells of 'Make a wish'.

Like he could get what he really wanted — to be good enough for Sergei and to have a family of his own. *That's not too much to wish for, is it?* Stuart had to blink back tears as he stole another quick glance at Sergei to see the man's brow furrowed in concern. Stuart spun around and reached for the small plates he had gotten out for the cake. "Did I see you brought ice cream to go with this?"

Lee went to the freezer to pull out the container he had stashed there. "Yep. We got vanilla, because we figured everyone would be okay with it. Where's your ice-cream scoop?"

Stuart pointed in the direction of the drawer holding all his miscellaneous kitchen utensils.

Lee pulled out the scoop and placed it next to the tub of ice cream. "Dude, your kitchen is the most squared away one I've ever seen. You have organizers for everything. Please tell me you have at least one junk drawer."

Stuart pointed to the drawer next to the refrigerator. Lee strode over and yanked it open, only to spin back around and point a finger at him. "Your junk drawer has an organizer. Who does that?"

"Um, people who want to be able to find things, maybe? I hate not being able to find something when I need it."

"I'm that way at the shop, but not in the kitchen," Kirk said while walking over to peek at the offending drawer.

"You don't cook," Eric scoffed. "Or should I say *can't*?"

"Either is true." Kirk shrugged, clearly not in the least offended by Eric's statement. "What about you, Sergei?"

"I can cook, but I don't have much time for it. I am quite busy with my many businesses. My housekeeper prepares meals and leaves them for me."

Chapter Two

Stuart's shoulders slumped after he'd spoken of his housekeeper and Sergei wondered why. Stuart looked away, being very careful not to make eye contact. They had gotten along so well at the wedding. Sergei had been completely charmed by Stuart. Now, Stuart seemed to be trying to keep him at arm's length. He hadn't even sat next to him during dinner, choosing instead to sit with the girls at the breakfast bar. Sergei was very interested to hear the story of why Stuart's family hadn't remembered his birthday. One thing Sergei didn't lack was nosy family members.

Sergei moved to stand next to Stuart, making sure to brush shoulders with him. Stuart used the excuse of handing him a piece of cake with ice cream to put some distance between them, almost shoving the cake into Sergei's chest in the process. Sergei stared at the cake then looked at Stuart, raising an eyebrow in inquiry.

"Sorry. I didn't realize you were so close."

"Now that's a lie, but I will let it go for now. We will discuss what I've done to upset you once the others have left. For now, enjoy your party." Sergei took his cake and went back to his seat at the table, next to Lee, as Stuart was called into the living room to set up a game for the girls on one of his gaming systems.

Lee mumbled something after he sat down, but Sergei didn't catch what it was. "Pardon?"

Lee spoke just a little bit louder, obviously trying to keep it low enough that Stuart couldn't hear him from the other room. "I said, he thinks you're out of his league. He doesn't know what you could see in him."

Sergei laughed, only to realize from Lee's stare that he was serious. "Really?"

Lee waved a hand indicating Sergei's suit. "You wore a suit to a birthday party at his house."

"And? It is what I wore today, as I had a meeting at the bank and did not have time to change. What does it matter?"

Lee blew out an exasperated breath. "Let's try this another way. How much did you pay for your suit?"

"Ten thousand dollars. What does that have to do with anything?"

Lee choked on the sip of soda he'd just taken. "You spent ten thousand dollars on a suit?"

"Yes, why? It's custom."

Lee waved his hand in front of his face. "Never mind, but jeebus, that's a lot of money for a suit." Shaking his head, Lee continued. "How many ten-thousand-dollar suits do you own?"

"I don't know…six or seven. I have a few more expensive ones too and several less expensive. Again, what does that have to do with anything?"

"You're sitting in Stuart's fourteen hundred square foot home, which he was able to purchase with the help of an inheritance from his uncle and money he had saved. He was able to get the house for eighty thousand dollars only because it needed a lot of work, which he's done most of himself to save money."

Sergei still didn't get Lee's point and it obviously showed, because Lee huffed out another breath and continued explaining. "You've spent more on suits than he has on his home."

Sergei was affronted. "I'm not a snob. It's a good home. It's like Stuart in many ways from what I have seen of it—warm and welcoming. I've not always been rich. I've earned my money."

"I know that, but I've had a chance to get to know you. That's the part of you Stuart needs to see, not this persona you've developed. I had the same problem of not knowing what I had to offer when I first started dating Saul."

Sergei sat back, deep in thought. "You are saying I am too successful."

"No. I'm saying you don't need to act like a successful businessman all the time. He only talked to you at the wedding because he didn't know who you were."

"What?" Sergei almost yelled, causing everyone to look at them for a moment. "What?" he asked more quietly.

Lee laughed at him. "Don't be offended. Why would Stuart need to know who you are? He has his own business, which he does out of his house. He's kept his head down and worked since he was kicked out of his house at eighteen."

"For being gay?" Sergei asked, not really surprised.

"Actually, no. Him being gay had nothing to do with it. His stepfather kicked him out as soon as he graduated because he didn't want another man's child in his house anymore, but you need to hear the rest of the story from Stuart."

Sergei ran a hand down his face. "I do not understand what you are trying to tell me here."

"I'm telling you that Stuart talked to you at the wedding, first because you are attractive then continued talking to you because he found you interesting. Your money had nothing to do with it. If you try to flash your money at him, you won't even have a chance. That's not what Stuart is about."

"Okay. Then what do you suggest?"

"Woo him."

"But you just said not to flash my money at him."

A look of total exasperation crossed Lee's face.

"Let me try," Eric interrupted with a chuckle, clearly having overheard the conversation. "Stuart needs to be wooed, not with things but with emotion. He's very sensitive and very alone. He acts outgoing, but he really isn't. He is shy and always worried about overstaying his welcome. He has two really good friends, his college roommate and now Lee. He and Lee have become close friends because they have things in common, so they have things to talk about. It's harder for him with the rest of us, because he isn't good at small talk. We were very surprised to see him talking and laughing with you at the wedding. Connection is what he needs, but you hurt him by leaving the wedding without getting his number. Now, he isn't sure what to think."

They all abruptly stopped talking and turned to look at Stuart when he came back in the kitchen.

"Wow. Don't make it too obvious that you were talking about me."

Kirk was the first to recover. "We were giving Sergei the 'hurt you and he answers to us' speech."

"Really?" Stuart looked both horrified and pleased at the possibility. "You know I'm a grown man. I can look out for myself."

Lee stood up and went to Stuart, throwing his arm across his shoulders. "We know you can, but he needs to know we're looking out for you too."

That was when Sergei saw what they were talking about. The pleased shyness crossing Stuart's face was amazing to see. Sergei wanted Stuart to look at him like that more than anything he had ever wanted in his life. The intensity of the desire he felt was a little overwhelming at first, but he had never let fear stand in the way of anything he wanted. He wasn't going to start now, with who he had a feeling would be the love of his life. *Oh yes.* Stuart was going to be his.

Sergei realized they were all staring at him, waiting for his response, and he had to remember what they'd been talking about before answering. "Duly noted. I will do my best not to cause a need for any such conversations."

"Make sure you don't," Eric said while patting him on the shoulder. "I would hate to sic Mama V on you."

"Oh yes, Saul's Mama is a scary woman for sure, but then you have not yet met my mama." Sergei didn't try to hide his shiver. "The woman is only five feet tall, but she scares me more than anyone on this planet." Sergei waited for the laughter to end before continuing. "I will try very hard not to upset either female. This is my vow as the head of the Barinov family."

Saul pointed a finger at Sergei. "See? It's that shit right there that makes people think you are some sort of mob boss."

"I assure you I am not. I am only a businessman. Why is it any time someone different achieves success in this country, it must be through some sort of underhanded trickery? I do not understand this way of thinking."

Saul shrugged his shoulders. "It's the American way. Don't try to understand it. It will never make sense. It just is. It's like people not believing I'm gay because I'm an ex-football player. They believe only a certain type of person can be gay. We all know that gay comes in all different shapes, sizes and looks, because people come in all different shapes, sizes and looks. Not every straight guy or girl looks the same, either."

Eric picked up where he'd left off. "We can only live our lives and try to educate people as we go. By Saul coming out publicly, as he did last year, maybe there were some people who had ah-ha moments and realized the truth—or maybe saw someone who accepted himself."

"Wait. I thought all Russians in America were part of the mob. You mean they're not?" Kirk was only able to hold the serious look on his face for about ten seconds before he dissolved into laughter.

"No," Sergei said dryly. "Not all Russians are part of the mob. Most just try to stay out of the way. Why am I friends with you people again?"

"Because we're not afraid of you," Saul said before laughing.

Sergei rolled his eyes at his friend before turning back to the cake in front of him. "Eric, this is delicious cake." For some reason, the comment made everyone laugh uproariously. "What? It's true."

Stuart came to his rescue. "Yes, now moving on to a new subject... Eric makes delicious cake. Thank you for doing it."

"Not a problem. It's a crowd favorite for sure, but we really do need to get going. It's a school night after all." Speaking a little louder to be heard in the next room, "Girls, wrap it up. It's time to go."

Good-natured grumbling came from the other room, but the girls soon appeared in the kitchen, carrying their dessert plates. "Do we have to go so soon?" Claire asked. "I like this house."

"You like Stuart's gaming system." Kirk reached out and bopped Claire on the nose. "Now come on. Shoes. School tomorrow."

"And make sure you tell Stuart happy birthday."

"Happy birthday, Stuart!" The girls spoke in unison then broke into giggles as they came to either side of him and gave him a hug.

"Are you coming to our soccer game on Saturday?" Sam asked.

"I don't know. What time is it?"

"Early. Eight-thirty," Eric answered with a grimace.

"Sure. I can be there. Lee and I aren't leaving until ten."

"Are you going to come too, Uncle Lee?"

Lee shot Stuart a look promising retribution. "Yeah. I was going to sleep in, but I guess I can come to your game. Stuart and I can leave from there."

"Yay!" The girls jumped up and down in their excitement before they were herded out of the door by Eric and Kirk.

"It's at the same place as usual. Field three. Happy birthday. See you Saturday," Eric said as he walked out of the door.

Lee went up and gave Stuart a hug. "You get to buy lunch since you got us roped into going to the soccer game. You couldn't think of an excuse?"

"I'll buy lunch, but I didn't hear you coming up with a reason to say no. Did you see those puppy-dog eyes?"

Lee sighed. "I know. They get me every time. Happy birthday, Stuart. I'll see you Saturday."

"Bright and early," Stuart answered with a grin.

"Don't remind me." Lee groaned loudly before heading out of the door with Saul following behind him. With a final 'happy birthday' from Saul, Sergei was finally alone with Stuart.

Stuart turned toward him, and Sergei found himself staring into his deep chocolate brown eyes for a moment before Stuart turned his back and got busy cleaning up the cake mess.

"You don't have to stay. There's not much left to do. I'm sure you're very busy."

Sergei came up behind him and wrapped his arms around Stuart. "I am not too busy for you. In case I did not make my intentions clear, I am very interested in you. I deeply regret that I failed to get your number before I left the wedding those weeks ago. I also deeply regret that I did not search you out sooner, since now you doubt our connection."

Sergei felt a shudder go through Stuart then had to strain to hear the whispered, "Why?"

"Why what?"

"Why would you be interested in me? I am *so* not in your league."

"Do you not feel our connection too?"

"Yeah, but…"

Sergei tightened his arms around Stuart. "The connection is what is important. The people involved are who are important. I don't even know this 'league' you speak about."

Stuart turned his head to look at Sergei, staring into his eyes and obviously trying to decide how sincere he was. "That's easy for you to say. You're the star player in the league. I'm the kid nobody picks who is sitting on the sideline."

Sergei grabbed Stuart's shoulder and turned him around so they were face to face. Leaning in, he pressed some of his weight into Stuart, holding him against the counter. "And yet I see you, and I am picking you." Sergei watched Stuart furrow his eyebrows and bite his lip. "Say what it is you want to say."

"How long?"

"How long what?"

"How long will you pick me? One night? Is that what you're looking for?"

"No. I'm not looking for just one night. As I said, we have a connection. I would really like to see where this connection takes us."

"Exclusively?"

"Why? Are you dating others?" Sergei growled the question, not liking the idea of anyone else dating Stuart at all.

Stuart barked out a laugh. "Hardly. You're the one photographed with a different person on your arm every week."

"I am told you didn't know who I was at the wedding. Did you google me?" Sergei was charmed by the blush rising up Stuart's face. "Ah-h." Sergei relaxed, putting more of his weight against Stuart. "To answer your question, I will only date you and you will only date me, until such time as we decide differently together." Sergei held up his hand to stop Stuart from speaking. "So that you are aware, I don't plan on that being any time soon, if ever. I am a man who knows what I want when I see it, and I am rarely wrong in my instincts. I'm sorry that I left you because I had to deal with my sister's latest crisis." Sergei paused to roll his eyes and shake his head at the thought of his sister. "My sister is a whole other topic. My mother wishes to meet you."

"Your *mother*? Why would your mother want to meet *me*?" Stuart's voice went up at the end in a bit of a squeak that Sergei found adorable.

"Because my mother is wise, and when I went to her home for brunch on Sunday, the day after the wedding, I was telling her about you and she said she was so happy I had found my person — and that she couldn't wait to meet you."

Stuart's eyes were getting bigger and bigger the longer Sergei talked.

"What? You do know that you sound like a crazy person, right?" Stuart pushed his way out of Sergei's arms and walked to the living room, where he started to pace. "Taking one look and knowing you met your person." Stuart put the word 'person' in air quotes and continued to pace. "Acting like you know you are going to keep me. *No one* keeps me."

"What does that mean?"

Stuart seemed to realize what he had said once Sergei asked the question, because he stopped pacing and stared at him for a moment before looking up at the ceiling.

"Are you looking for the answer up there?" Sergei snuck a peek to see if he had missed something. *Nope. Just a ceiling.*

"Ah-h-h." Stuart screamed and grabbed his hair, pulling a moment before dropping his hands and turning to look Sergei in the eye. "You're making me crazy."

"Why? For wanting to understand what you meant?"

"Yes."

Sergei studied Stuart, waiting for him to explain further. When he realized nothing else was coming, he prodded, "Why is it making you crazy that I want to understand you?"

"Because I'm not interesting enough."

"I find you fascinating."

"Like a bug, maybe. I'm a squashed bug on the windshield, aren't I?" There was a decisive nod from Stuart, as if that were truly the answer, before he started pacing again.

Sergei reached out and grabbed Stuart on one of his trips past, pulling him into his arms and kissing him senseless, not stopping until Stuart sagged in his arms. Raising his head from the kiss, he waited for Stuart to open his eyes and look at him before speaking.

"I do not think you are a bug. I think you are an absolutely fascinating human being. You were able to converse with me for an hour about many subjects at the wedding. Do you know how rare that is?" He did not wait for an answer this time. "Tomorrow night, I wish to take you to dinner. Say yes to me."

"Yes."

Sergei was pleased to see that Stuart still seemed to be struggling to recover from the kiss.

"Good." Leaning down, he stole another kiss before stepping back and taking Stuart's hand in his. "I shall plan to pick you up at six o'clock. Does that work for you?"

"Um-m, yes." Stuart shook his head as if trying to make sense of it all. "It should be fine. I have a meeting at three, but it should only take an hour or so."

"Good. Then tomorrow, I will start the wooing."

"Wooing? Why would you woo me?"

"Because I have never met anyone who needed wooing more."

"You do remember I'm a guy, right?"

"What does that have to do with anything?" Sergei raised an eyebrow at him in question. "I am well aware you are a guy. It does not matter, male or female. You will still be wooed, as is proper."

"Who the hell uses the word 'wooing'?" Stuart threw his hands in the air in obvious frustration.

"I do. Prepare to be wooed." Leaning in, he gave Stuart another hard kiss before turning and heading to the door. Stopping with his hand on the doorknob, he turned back toward Stuart. "Dress casual. Jeans are fine."

"Do you even own jeans?"

"Of course I own jeans. I am an American now." Shaking his head at Stuart, Sergei turned to let himself out of the house.

Mama will be so happy. I can't wait to tell her.

Chapter Three

Stuart stood inside his walk-in closet, staring at his selection of shirts and hoping something would jump out at him as the perfect choice. Honestly, he owned a lot of T-shirts and some business attire for meetings. He didn't have a lot in between. That was what happened when someone worked from home. Somehow, he didn't think 'casual' to Sergei extended to T-shirts. *Oh well*. He'd start as he meant to go on. Sergei had said casual. Stuart reached out and grabbed his favorite one from its hanger. It was one of the many given to him by his best friend Paul. He then grabbed a short-sleeved collared shirt to put over it, leaving the buttons undone. If they ended up going somewhere that didn't appreciate the mouse, he could always button the shirt.

Running his hand through his hair, he looked into the full-length mirror he'd had installed in his closet. It was as good as he was getting. The doorbell rang before he could obsess any more. He gave himself a pep talk as he walked. *One date*. Sergei would realize how truly boring he was, then he could get on with his life. With a decisive nod to himself, Stuart reached out and opened the door, only to be rendered speechless when he saw Sergei.

He was dressed in well-worn jeans, biker boots and one of those tight wicking T-shirts that molded to his body like a second skin. Over the T-shirt, he had on a black leather jacket. He looked totally badass and Stuart found that he had to swallow hard to stop from drooling all over himself. Stuart ran another full body scan down to Sergei's boot-clad feet then up to Sergei's face, only to find Sergei smirking at him when he got there.

Sergei looked down at himself then back at Stuart with a spark of amusement in his eyes. "Like what you see?"

Stuart rolled his eyes at Sergei so hard that it almost hurt. "Of course I do. You're a stunning man."

Sergei stepped closer, grabbed Stuart by the front of his shirt and pulled him in until they were pressed together from chest to groin. "As are you, *kotik*." Before Stuart could ask what *kotik* meant, Sergei pressed their lips together, placing his hand on the back of Stuart's head and positioning Stuart just as he wanted him. Sergei pressed for entry with his tongue and all Stuart could do was moan and let him in. Minutes or hours later—damned if Stuart knew—Sergei raised his head and stared down into Stuart's eyes. Stuart made himself step back and he waved a hand in the direction of the door. "Are you ready to go?"

"You will need a jacket, *kotik*, as I brought the convertible. It is a beautiful night for a drive."

Looking behind him, Stuart saw a Porsche 911 convertible with a custom paint job sitting with the top down in his driveway. "Oh wow. Did Lee do the paint work?"

"Who else?" Sergei answered with a shrug. "He is the best, after all."

"That he is." Stuart could only shake his head. "You might want to go wait outside with the car while I get my leather jacket. It's upstairs. My neighborhood is nice, but we don't get too many hundred-thousand-dollar cars around here."

"As you wish."

Heading up the stairs, Stuart risked a glance backward to find Sergei watching him. "What?"

"You're a very beautiful man and I enjoy watching you move."

"O-ka-a-ay," Stuart dragged out the word, beyond flustered at this point. His heart still hadn't settled down from the kiss. He took his time grabbing his jacket, taking deep breaths until he finally felt like he had a little bit of control over himself, only to have his heart start pounding again when he walked outside and saw Sergei leaning back against his car, looking like a model. Stuart had to swallow hard then hold his jacket in front of him so he could adjust himself with a little bit of subtlety. He obviously wasn't subtle enough, though, if Sergei's smirk was any indication.

Stuart attempted to hide his embarrassment by putting on his jacket. *What is it about this man that can wreck my composure just by him being within ten feet of me?* Glancing up at Sergei where he still leaned against his car, Stuart had his answer. *Oh yeah, he's a walking, talking sex god and the embodiment of every single one of the items on my dream-man wish list. Too bad I don't believe in dreams anymore. They always leave me disappointed.*

Sergei pushed off the car and went to open Stuart's door for him. "What a gentleman," Stuart said with a smile. He waited until Sergei went around the car and climbed into the driver's seat before asking, "Where are we going?"

"Well, I thought we would take a drive out to Jordan Lake. The weather is gorgeous tonight, especially for the end of September, and the sun will not set for another couple of hours. Then we'll have dinner afterward."

"Sounds good," Stuart said, running his hand over the dashboard as Sergei backed the car out of the drive. "I've never been in a Porsche before. This is amazing."

"She's my baby. I told myself when I was a teenager that one day I would own one. I would know I made it when I could pay cash for it."

Stuart couldn't help his chuckle. "Pay cash for a hundred-thousand-dollar-plus car? You set the bar pretty high, didn't you?"

Sergei shrugged while running his hands over the steering wheel. "And yet I achieved my goal. I'm kind of a big deal, you know."

"I didn't when we were talking at the wedding, to be honest. I was simply blown away by your beauty and your accent."

"My beauty?" Sergei scoffed. "I am not beautiful."

"You're strong and confident and intelligent, all things I find beautiful."

"Okay then, I will be beautiful for you." Sergei shot him a wicked grin as he spoke.

Stuart chuckled. "Thank you for accommodating me."

Sergei reached out, took Stuart's hand and raised it to his lips, placing a kiss on his knuckles. "I like accommodating you."

Stuart gently extricated his hand from Sergei's grip. "Just drive." Stuart watched Sergei smoothly shifting gears as they got onto the highway and picked up speed, admiring his strong hand on the gear shift. After a few minutes, Stuart closed his eyes and enjoyed the feel of the wind in his hair. Lifting his chin a little, he raised his face to the sun and let its rays warm him. Sergei reached out and placed his hand on Stuart's thigh, squeezing gently. Stuart shot Sergei a look before settling back in his seat a little more, closing his eyes again and simply being. It was a heady feeling. He opened his eyes and looked around when Sergei removed his hand and he heard the blinker turn on. Looking out of the window, he realized they were already exiting the highway.

"Wow. That was fast," Stuart said when they stopped at the stoplight before they would make the left turn on to highway 751, which would take them to the lake.

"I think you may have fallen asleep for a little bit." Turning to look at Sergei, Stuart found a smug look on his face.

"Why does me falling asleep make you so happy?" Stuart waved a hand in Sergei's direction.

"If you're able to sleep while I'm driving, it means you trust me."

"Well, yeah. Physically I trust you. I have no reason not to. You handle the car well."

"Yes, and we will work on you trusting me in all ways, but this is a good start, I think."

Stuart stared at him for a long moment, not knowing what to say. "Just drive, Barinov."

Sergei threw him another smirk as he made the turn then picked up speed, making it through the next light then passing a new subdivision being built.

Stuart raised his voice to be heard over the wind noise. "This part of town has changed so much over the last couple years. It used to all just be trees."

"Yeah, but it's the price of progress. I figured we would maybe go to the burger place at the mall here on our way back."

"Sounds good. The food there is fantastic."

"But that is for after. For now, enjoy the view." They had finally made it out of the congested area and were on the backcountry roads leading to the lake. Stuart looked out of the window and watched the trees pass by in a blur, followed by glimpses of the lake as they got closer. Sergei slowed and made the turn into the park on the north side of the man-made lake and water reservoir for the surrounding area.

"There is something so relaxing about the water. I am really looking forward to going to Wilmington on Saturday with Lee. The ocean is so powerful and ever moving, but there is something to be said about lakes too. They can be so still and calm, but then they can be choppy and rough, depending on the weather. They say that on calm days you can see the roofs of some of the houses they flooded when they made the lake." Stuart realized he was babbling and made himself stop talking.

"I didn't know about the houses."

Stuart gave a self-deprecating shrug. "I'm not sure if that's true or not, but it's what I heard."

Sergei swung his car into a parking spot and put the car in Park. "Come on. Let's go explore and find out what we can see today."

Stuart climbed out of the car and met Sergei at the rear of the vehicle, pleasantly surprised when Sergei reached out and took his hand before walking toward the lake.

The lake was calm and pretty empty of visitors on a Wednesday evening. Reaching the edge of the water, Sergei pulled Stuart in front of him with Stuart's back to his chest and wrapped his arms around him. "This is my thinking spot. Whenever I am struggling with a decision, I like to come here. Something about this place calms me."

"Do you have a decision to make?"

"Nope. I've never brought anyone else here, but I wanted to share it with you."

Stuart felt a flutter of something go through him. It took him a moment to identify the feeling as pleasure. Clearing the lump of emotion from his throat, he was able to respond. "It's a beautiful place."

Sergei tightened his arms around Stuart in response. The calm of the moment was broken by the sound of Sergei's phone ringing. A sense of déjà vu hit as Sergei excused himself to answer it.

Stuart could only hear Sergei's side of the conversation. "What is it, Natasha? No, I am not going to Sasha's game tonight. I told you that I have a date." Pause. "No, I will not be there. I told you this. I have been to many others. He can be without me for one night." Another pause. "I did *not* tell him I would be at the game and you *know* I'm on a date." Longer pause. "What do you mean your friend Evelyn brought someone for me to meet at the game because she thought I would be there? What do I care what Evelyn does or does not think? I do not report to Evelyn and neither do you."

Sergei made eye contact with Stuart and Stuart raised an eyebrow at him. "I do not wish to meet anyone else, Natasha. As you know, because *I told you*," Sergei emphasized the last part, "that I am already on a date, with someone I really like. Do *not* try to set me up anymore and spread the word that I am no longer available. Do not call me again tonight unless it is an emergency, Natasha."

Sergei pressed the button to end the phone call, only for the phone in his hand to start ringing again almost immediately. Sergei stared at the screen in disbelief before pressing the button to decline the call, silencing the phone and slipping it back into his pocket.

"Now, where were we?"

"I'm not sure, to be honest. Did you need to go to this Sasha's game?"

Sergei stood up taller and looked down his nose at Stuart. Stuart wished it wasn't such a turn on. He should be pissed, but man, haughty Sergei did something for him. He had to focus to hear what Sergei was saying.

"If I needed to be at my brother's game, I would not have scheduled a date with you tonight. I've been to many games. My brother doesn't even like playing soccer." Sergei threw his hands up in exasperation. "He only plays because his father used to play. He is more into his computers and such. He also likes acting. I make sure I go to his plays."

Stuart rolled his lips and pressed them together hard to hide his smile, holding his hands up in a placating gesture. "Okay, okay, I get it. You are a fantastic older brother. How old are your siblings?"

"Natasha turns twenty-one next month. She is a senior at the University of North Carolina at Chapel Hill. My brother is seventeen and a junior in high school."

"Wow. That's quite the age gap between you. You're what? Thirty-five?"

"Thirty-six, actually. There are fifteen years between me and Natasha. My mother was always very smart. She was in college at fifteen for mathematics and science. A professor sought to take advantage of her and steal her work. I was the result of the relationship."

"He raped her?" Stuart allowed the horror to show in his voice at the thought.

"No. My mother insists it was consensual, as much as a fifteen-year-old really understands when being pursued by her role model. Looking back, she certainly knows it wasn't right, but at the time, all she was concerned about was someone who would feed her and look out for her. You have to understand that the age of consent in Russia at the time was fourteen, so there was nothing legally wrong with them having a relationship. She came from a farming family in a very poor village, and while book-smart, she was quite naïve. She went along with it when he said people couldn't know about him and told her she couldn't put his name on my birth certificate because people would talk. He set us up in a small apartment not far from the university while Mom continued her undergraduate then two graduate degrees in chemistry then mathematics.

"She was so busy between me and her studies that she did not realize he was using her until she overheard some people talking in his office about Pyotr's wife being so excited about him winning a prestigious science award for a paper he had published. As the paper was my mother's work and they had never married, my mother was very confused and decided to investigate. She found out that not only was he married with two children, but he had also published her work under his name. She was furious."

"Understandably so," Stuart responded.

"She had already applied to schools in the United States to get her doctorate and had never understood why he had always discouraged her from doing so. She had been on her way to tell him that she had been accepted at Duke and was being offered a stipend and a fellowship to boot. Instead, she went to our small apartment and worked on all the visa paperwork with a lawyer she knew. It was an advantage that she had not listed Pyotr as my father on the birth certificate. He had no say in me going with her. A few months later, we were in the United States."

"How old were you then?"

"Nine. I came to this country knowing what I thought was a lot of English. My mother was fairly fluent, but there is a difference between having conversations when you can switch back to Russian at any time and having to speak English all the time. It was exhausting."

"I can imagine. I struggled to get through the required two years of Spanish that I needed to take in high school. Languages are *so* not my thing." Stuart chuckled when Sergei did.

"It was not all bad. I was good at sports. I made friends easily enough and I worked hard to learn English."

"Okay. So, then what happened? Obviously, she met someone."

"Yes." Sergei smiled, obviously thinking back. "She met Sean Hamilton. He was a fellow doctoral student who was studying history. He's now a professor. He lived in the same apartment complex that we did. He was so nice to us. We didn't have a lot of money. He started showing up with pizza or burgers, pretending it was to have a quiet place to study as he shared a two-bedroom apartment with three others to save money."

"Pretending?"

"Well, he really just wanted an excuse to talk to my mom and get to know her. They were friends first, then they started dating."

"Is she like you? Did she know he was going to be her person?"

Sergei gave Stuart a grin. "Yes. She knew almost immediately that he was her person, but she was wary after everything with Pyotr. I mean, she knew Pyotr wasn't her one, but she had been willing to settle in order to feel not so alone."

"It makes sense," Stuart said with a shrug. "She was fifteen and in college by herself."

"Exactly."

"And do you like your stepfather?"

"I love him. He's a wonderful human being. A bit of a nerd and a scatterbrain, but he's a great person. He adores my mother, worships the ground she walks on."

"As he should."

"As he should," Sergei agreed.

Stuart paused for a moment to think. "Does your sister not want you to be gay? I mean, you said she knew you were on a date, but then why was she still trying to get you to come to the game and meet someone tonight?"

Sergei scoffed. "It has nothing to do with me dating a man. I have dated both women and men in the past."

"Then why is she trying to get you to leave your date with me and go meet someone else?"

"Some Evelyn woman claims Natasha told her I would be there tonight and made a big deal over the fact that she brought her poor, recently divorced sister to meet me — or some such nonsense."

"Okay, I guess it makes sense that she would call to see if your plans had changed tonight, but explain why was it necessary for you to leave the wedding? Your stepfather is still alive, isn't he?"

"Yes. Quite. Natasha called me because her car had broken down."

"Why did she call *you* then? Did she not know you had plans?"

"I have always looked out for Natasha, and yes, she knew I had plans."

"Why would it mean she had to call you? Were your parents doing something that evening?"

"No. They were at home."

Stuart took a step back from Sergei as his anger flared again. "Let me get this straight. You answered a call at the wedding from Natasha and left me in the middle of a conversation when her parents were at home to help her."

"Was that a question? You know that is what happened. Is this back to the leaving the wedding without getting your number? I've already apologized for that." Sergei looked like he was getting frustrated, so Stuart took a moment to organize his thoughts.

"Yes, you did apologize for leaving without getting my number, but I thought we were having a moment here. You allowed your sister to interrupt us again. She has other people in her life she can contact. Why couldn't you let us have the moment? If I'm your person, shouldn't I be a priority?"

Sergei opened his mouth then closed it again without saying anything before crossing to Stuart and pulling him into his arms in a strong hug. Stuart hesitated a moment before lifting his arms and placing them around Sergei's waist to hug him back.

"Not that I'm complaining, but what's the hug for?"

"For making me listen. You are wise. Sean has said something similar from time to time. I did not understand what he meant."

"What has Sean said?"

"He has said many times that he wishes I would let him be the hero sometimes. Natasha always comes to me first, but he always laughs about it after, so I never really gave it much thought." Sergei pecked a kiss to

Stuart's lips before continuing. "You're right. I should not have let her interrupt our moment."

"Not if you meant the moment to be special. No, you shouldn't have."

"Agreed. I can see where that came across as disrespectful to you." A mischievous look came into Sergei's eyes. "Look! We've had our first fight. Time to make up." Sergei lowered his head and took Stuart's mouth in a ravenous kiss. He pressed his tongue between Sturt's lips and twined their tongues together, while at the same time pulling his body tighter against him.

Stuart's head whirled with the onslaught. Their chemistry was definitely off the charts. When Sergei pulled back, Stuart slowly opened his eyes to find Sergei staring at him. Stuart felt himself flush and tried to pull away, but Sergei was having none of it.

"No. Stay close. Let me hold you a moment longer." Sergei pulled Stuart back into his arms and pushed Stuart's head down to rest on his shoulder. They stood quietly together until their breathing evened out.

The moment was broken by the growl of Stuart's stomach in hunger. Sergei shook with laughter. "Are you hungry perhaps, *kotik*?"

"Yeah. I'm starving, actually. What does *kotik* mean? You keep calling me that."

"It means 'kitten'."

Stuart was torn between horror and amusement. "Kitten? Why would you call me *kitten*?"

"Because you remind me of this stray kitten I found once behind a dumpster. It hissed and tried to scratch me when I was trying to catch it because being alone and scared was what it knew, but really all it wanted or needed was to have someone take care of it."

Stuart stepped back and crossed his arms over his chest. "I'm not scared, and I certainly don't need anyone to take care of me."

Sergei chuckled. "Nope. You're terrified, but I tamed Oscar and I will woo you until you are comfortable with me too."

"Wait! You named a cat you found behind a garbage can Oscar?"

"Yes. It seemed appropriate. No?"

Their conversation was interrupted by another loud growl from Stuart's stomach.

"The next step is to feed you, I think." Sergei held out his hand to Stuart. "Come. Let's get some dinner."

Stuart reluctantly took Sergei's hand, grumbling as they walked. "I am *so* not a kitten. A tiger maybe, but not a kitten."

"Whatever you say, *kotik*."

"And you are *so* not funny."

Chapter Four

Sergei chuckled to himself as he opened the passenger door for Stuart and watched him sit and buckle himself in before closing the door and walking around to get into the driver's seat and do the same. While what he had told Stuart was true, he could have also told him that he reminded him of a cat when he walked — all smooth grace and caution. He loved to watch Stuart move. In fact, watching him dance on the dance floor at Kirk and Eric's wedding had been what had prompted him to seek him out at the open bar, when he'd stopped dancing to get a drink. He had been further intrigued when Stuart's mind had proven to be just as impressive as his dance moves.

Sergei put the car in gear and headed back the way they had come, to the mall just off the highway. There was an easy silence between them as they made the trip. Pulling into the parking lot closest to the restaurant where they were going, Sergei lucked into a spot right up front.

"Man, I usually end up parking in the back of nowhere whenever I come here. You are one lucky guy."

Sergei chuckled. "Maybe you're my good luck charm."

Stuart rolled his eyes at Sergei. "Yeah, whatever. Let's go eat. I'm starving." Stuart's stomach echoed the sentiment with another loud growl. They exited the car and met in front. Sergei took Stuart's hand in his again as they started walking toward the restaurant.

"I made reservations for eight o'clock." Sergei glanced down at the watch on his wrist. "We're only a few minutes early. Hopefully our table will be ready soon."

"I hope so."

"Did you not have lunch?" Sergei growled when he realized Stuart was actually having to think about it. "At least tell me you had breakfast."

"Um, does coffee and a granola bar count?"

Sergei stopped and glared at Stuart for a moment. "No. Coffee and a granola bar don't count if you don't eat lunch."

Stuart shrugged before pulling on Sergei's hand to get him started walking again. "I got a phone call from a client right when I was going to go make some lunch, then by the time I was off the call, it was time to head to my meeting and I forgot."

"You need a keeper, *kotik*."

Stuart chuckled, obviously getting over his earlier irritation. "Well, it seems you have already applied for the job, mob-man."

"I am *not* a mobster," Sergei grumbled before stepping up and giving his name to the young woman at the hostess stand. "Reservation for Barinov."

"Yes, sir. Right this way." The perky young woman led the way to a table on the outside covered patio. Once they were both seated, she left them with the menus.

"Would you like to share a bottle of wine?" Sergei asked while looking over the separate drink menu.

"I'm not really much of a wine drinker. Would you be interested in splitting a milkshake instead?"

Sergei looked up at Stuart in surprise before grinning in delight. "I would love to share a milkshake with you. It is such a stereotypical American thing to do on a date."

Stuart chuckled. "They actually split milkshakes here into two glasses, but if you want to share a milkshake with two straws, we can do that too."

"Yes, let's do it. What kind do you want?"

"I usually get the crème brûlée or plain strawberry. I'm really kind of a purist when it comes to my food. I like simple."

"Well, simple it is. Let's get the strawberry."

After the food and drink orders were placed, they stared at each other for a few moments before Stuart chuckled and broke the connection. He took off his jacket and Sergei watched as his muscles flexed under the T-shirt and shirt he wore. Licking his lips, he looked up to find Stuart smirking at him.

"See something you like?" Stuart said, throwing back Sergei's earlier question at him.

"Oh yes." Sergei took his turn taking his jacket off and placing it on the back of his chair. As he did so, his phone fell out of the pocket with a clatter and he leaned down to pick it up. The phone vibrated in his hand and he glanced at it before putting the phone face down on the table with a grimace.

"Something wrong?"

"No. It just shows that I have a bunch of text messages from my sister. I don't think she is pleased with me."

"You can answer her. I'm not saying you can't communicate with her, just not when we're having a moment."

Sergei stared at Stuart, trying to see if he meant it.

"I'm serious," Stuart said with a chuckle. "I know you're a successful businessman and that your family is important to you. I know you're busy and I'm not wanting to get between you and your family, but if we're going to date, I need to know I have a place too. I can't be the one who gets your leftover time."

"That makes sense, and please know that you *are* a priority. My family will have to learn to share me." Just then, Sergei's screen lit up with another incoming text. "Oh, for goodness sake."

"Go ahead," Stuart said with a wave in the phone's direction. "See what's going on."

Sergei picked up his phone to look at the ten text messages he had from his sister and the one message from his assistant, Brandon. He started with the one from Brandon. "Oh good. Brandon was able to schedule a meeting for tomorrow with the owner of the bar I'm looking to purchase."

"Who's Brandon?" Stuart leaned back as he asked the question so their server could set the large strawberry shake between them. "We'll need a second straw when you get a chance."

The server blinked at Stuart for a moment then glanced at Sergei before giving them both a brilliant smile and reaching into her apron pocket. "Of course. Here you go."

Stuart opened both straws and stuck them in the milkshake, one on each side, before leaning over to take a sip. "Man, that's good. Sorry, where were we? Oh yeah. Who's Brandon?"

Sergei leaned forward for his own taste of milkshake and was pleasantly surprised by the flavor. "Wow. That *is* good. I can't remember the last time I had a milkshake. Brandon is my personal assistant and right-hand man. I hired him straight out of college, and he has worked his way into his current role with the company. I truly don't know what I would do without him now."

Stuart grinned at him before continuing the conversation. "It's great you have someone you can count on."

"It really is."

"Which bar are you wanting to purchase?"

"Puzzles."

"The place that has the game rooms and pool tables and such?"

"Yeah. I heard a rumor that the owner is looking to sell. It's a fantastic location."

"I like that bar. It's a great place to chill, the food's decent and it's quite popular."

"Yep. Which is why, when I heard the rumor, that I wanted to get right on it."

"Cool. Out of curiosity, what does your sister have to say?"

"I don't know yet." Sergei admitted with a wince. "She has sent me ten texts. They're probably not good things." He picked up the phone again and looked at the messages. He chuckled as he read through. "Let's just say she isn't happy with me for hanging up—and leave it at that."

"Upset as only a twenty-one-year-old can be?"

"Oh yes." Sergei sent a quick text to his sister, before setting the phone face-down on the table once more and turning to look at his date again.

"What did you say?"

"I told her I would talk to her later."

"Oh man. She is going to blow up your phone with texts now."

"And calls too, probably," Sergei allowed with a smirk. "Let's change the subject. I know you're going to Wilmington on Saturday for lunch with Lee. Any plans for the evening?"

"Looking to schedule date two before we even finish date one?"

"As it is only Wednesday, I am hoping we can schedule another date between now then and that would make it date three, actually."

"Ah, looking for a sleepover?"

Sergei reached out and took Stuart's hand in his, making sure to maintain eye contact. "I do not doubt our chemistry, but a sleepover will only happen when you're comfortable with me. I personally have had enough one-night stands. I am looking for something more with you."

Stuart looked down and stared at the milkshake for a moment before locking gazes with Sergei again. "We agreed we were going to date exclusively. This is already not a one-night stand. Right?"

"Right."

"I honestly don't think we will do ourselves any favors with chemistry like ours if we hold off on the physical aspect of our relationship. Condoms are a requirement for me, until our window is long enough for us to get tested together."

Sergei released the breath he had been holding as he'd waited to see where Stuart was going with his train of thought. "Okay, but not tonight. Tonight is about getting to know each other better. Tomorrow night I will bring takeout and clothes for work on Friday."

Stuart swallowed visibly and shot Sergei a crooked grin. "Building the anticipation?"

"Oh, I will not be leaving you needing tonight, *kotik*. Not now, when I have been given a green light." He chuckled at the visible shiver that went through Stuart's body. "I simply was not prepared for a sleepover."

The food arrived and Sergei leaned back in his chair, releasing Stuart's hand so the server could place the food on the table. The server placed the basket of fries in the middle for them to share and put each of their burgers in front of them. They grinned and talk was sidelined as they dug into their meals. Long minutes later, Sergei sat back with a loud exhale and responded to Stuart's questioning look.

"There is something so satisfying about a good burger and fries sometimes. I mean, I like a good steak as much as the next person, but a good burger after a busy day can be so amazing."

"Careful there. Your American is showing," Stuart said with a smirk.

Sergei scoffed. "Make no mistake… I have a strong Russian core, but I am definitely an American. There is so much here that it would be easy to let my past go, but I will never forget where I came from. Don't get me wrong. I enjoy where I am and have no desire to ever go back, especially as Russia is not very welcoming to homosexuals, no matter how much money one does or does not have."

The grin slid off Stuart's face. "I didn't mean to offend you."

"Oh, you didn't, *kotik*. I simply meant that many people think that in order to be American you must give up what makes you not American. I embrace all parts."

"America is definitely not one size fits all."

"No, but there are those who wish to make it that way."

"Americans definitely like their stereotypes."

"It's not only Americans. I think people in general want things to make sense—to follow the rules, so to speak, even if those rules are completely arbitrary."

"We were talking about that the other night about how gay is supposed to look and act a certain way."

"Exactly. Neither of us are stereotypical gay males."

"I don't feel like I'm a very good gay, actually," Stuart said with a self-deprecating laugh.

"What do you mean? How can one be a 'bad' gay? Have you hurt other people or pretended to be something you are not?"

"No. That's not it. It's just... How do I explain this...?" Stuart trailed off as he obviously tried to organize his thoughts. "I've never really paid much attention to gay issues, to be honest. I had to work so hard after I was kicked out of my family home at eighteen. I worked three jobs during breaks and at least one during school to pay for everything. I had a dream to own my own business and make enough money so I would never be left with nothing—or virtually nothing—again."

Stuart held up a hand to stop Sergei as he opened his mouth to respond. "Don't get me wrong, I was lucky from the standpoint that at least I had my uncle to live with over the summer and breaks, so I wasn't completely homeless, and I had a fantastic roommate all four years of college. I simply tried to keep my head above water and live my life. I didn't have time to go to gay bars, date, become involved in protests or even really pay attention to the issues. I didn't have time to watch RuPaul's show, and while I have mad respect for drag queens and have gone to a few shows, I have no desire to wear make-up. I've never even been to a Pride parade."

"I have a cousin, Nikolai, who is very much the twink, gay stereotype from the makeup-wearing to the show-watching, but I had no desire to do any of that either. To be honest, Nikolai kind of scares me. He's one of the smartest people I know, currently at college completing his doctorate in finance. He has been giving me financial advice since he was fifteen. Great advice, I should say. Nikolai is absolutely amazing and doesn't care what anyone thinks of him — or at least that's how he comes across." He paused as a thought came to him. "Except when he is in the same room as Brandon."

"Your assistant?"

"Yeah. Whenever Brandon is around, Nikolai becomes this clumsy, awkward and strangely shy person who I don't recognize."

"Oh. Sounds like he has a crush."

Sergei felt a rush of surprise. "You think so?"

"Yeah. It definitely sounds it."

"Hm-m. I will have to give the idea some thought and observe closer. Anyway, my point is, how someone looks on the outside has no bearing on who or what they are."

"You're preaching to the choir. My college roommate is a prime example of that. He is this super geeky, Asian-American artist and everyone assumed he was gay."

"He's not?"

"Nope. He fell in love with his now-wife Chloe in college. She's his everything. She's this gorgeous redhead who is four inches taller than him, but they just work together. She grounds him and he reminds her to play."

"That's very nice. Speaking of playing, if you wish to attend a Pride parade, we can certainly do so any time you want."

"I know. I could have gone to a parade at any time over the last five years if I'd wanted, but I really don't want to go. I hate crowds. I mean, I *really* hate crowds. I want to live my life and find someone to share it with. I know I can only have this because of all the others who spoke up and followed through. I greatly appreciate all those people. It's just not me."

"I haven't done as much as I could, if those are your criteria for what makes a good or bad gay person. The same could be said for most Americans, though." Sergei shrugged. "I donate money to LGBT causes and I have acceptance policies in place at all of my businesses. Maybe we could look at doing more together."

It was Stuart's turn to shrug. "Maybe. It might be fun."

Their server came up to refill their water glasses and Sergei took the opportunity to request the check.

"Unless you wanted something else?" Sergei arched an eyebrow at Stuart in inquiry.

"Not at all. I'm stuffed." Addressing their server, "Everything was great. Thank you."

"No problem, gentlemen. Here's your check."

Sergei glanced at the total and put in enough cash to cover the check and a generous tip.

"Shall we go?" Sergei grabbed Stuart's hand and held it as they made their way out the side gate off the patio to Sergei's car. Stuart waved him off when they reached the hood of the car.

"Just get in. The sooner you get in, the sooner we can get home."

After he was seated and started the car, he turned his head to look at Stuart. "Anywhere else you would like to go?"

"No. Take me home, Sergei. I do believe we have some unfinished business." Stuart ran his hand up the inside of Sergei's thigh, pausing just before he made contact with his hardening cock.

"Home it is. Much as it pains me to say this, you need to keep your hands to yourself so I can concentrate." Sergei put the car in gear, once Stuart had moved his hand, drove out of the parking lot and headed to Stuart's house. He turned his head to find Stuart staring at him. "What?"

"I'm trying to figure out what I did to get you as a boyfriend. You're gorgeous and successful. I mean, I'm successful to a point. I have everything I need, but I'm certainly not gorgeous. I'm kinda average."

Sergei was shocked. "There is nothing average about you. You're stunning." Sergei shot another look in Stuart's direction. "You have to know that."

"I'm already gonna sleep with you. You don't have to lay on the flattery. I know what I look like."

"Your mirror is obviously faulty if you think I am being anything but honest. You're gorgeous."

Their discussion was interrupted by Sergei's phone ringing through the Bluetooth in the car. Natasha's name flashed up on the display screen, causing Sergei to grimace.

"You might as well take it. Make sure she knows I'm in the car, though. I would rather you get it over with so she doesn't interrupt us later."

With a sigh, Sergei hit the button to answer the phone. "Natasha, I am in the car with Stuart, still on my date. I told you I would call you later."

"This isn't about that. Sasha got hurt. Mom and Dad are taking him to the emergency room."

"What? What happened."

"He collided with another player. They think his arm is broken." Sarcasm laced her voice as she added. "I figured maybe you would want to know, even if you *are* on a date." With a condescending sniff, Natasha hung up.

"I'm sorry. Let me call my mama and see what is happening."

"Of course."

Sergei hit the button on the screen to connect a call to his mother. The phone rang twice before his mother's heavily accented voice came over the line.

"I thought you were on a date. Why are you calling me?" The matter-of-fact way his mother spoke calmed him immediately.

"Natasha called and said Sasha was hurt and you were taking him to the hospital."

"That girl. I told her not to bother you. Your father and I are driving Sasha to the orthopedic urgent care now." There was a pause and Sergei heard someone else speaking but couldn't make out their words, only his mother's response. "Natasha called Sergei. Yes, I know we told her not to bother him. She is going to have to learn to share his attention. You must speak with her, Sean. Perhaps she will listen to you." Back on the phone with Sergei. "Sergei, Sasha will be fine. He has had worse. At least it is not his head this time. One more concussion this year and he would not be able to play anymore."

"I'm fine, bro," came from the background, causing both Sergei and Stuart to chuckle.

"Is Stuart in the car with you?" his mother asked.

"Yes, ma'am. I'm here," Stuart confirmed

"Good. Then you can hear this too and maybe make Sergei believe it. Natasha is not the center of the universe and he doesn't have to cater to her every whim. She is turning into quite a brat and I will not have it." Stuart chuckled and shot Sergei a look as Sergei winced. "It is good Sergei has met someone. He has told me much about you and I look forward to meeting you."

"Thank you. I look forward to meeting you too." Stuart's response was quiet and there was an underlayer of fear in his voice that surprised Sergei.

"Good. You will come to dinner Sunday. Right, Sergei?"

"*Da*, Mama. We will be there."

"Good. Six o'clock. I will call later and let you know about your brother."

"Thank you, Mama."

"Now go. Enjoy the rest of your date."

"Yes, Mama."

Stuart was laughing as Sergei hung up the phone. "What is so funny?"

"You. At my birthday party you said your mother terrified you. I thought you were kidding, but you really weren't."

"No. Not at all. My mother is quite fierce. She had to learn to be." Sergei reached out and grabbed Stuart's hand. "I promise you that my family life is not usually so crazy."

"It's all good. It's nice to see a family who cares about one another so much. Saul's and Eric's families are tight too. I've been privileged to be included in a lot of events with them."

"But not your own?"

"Nah, but that's okay. I have the guys and I have my college roommate Paul and his family."

Sergei didn't really believe it was all right, but he let the subject drop as he pulled into Stuart's driveway.

"Listen. Why don't you drop me off tonight and go find your family? Maybe have it out with your sister. I don't think you're in the right mindset to come in. I don't want our first time to be with your head full of other people."

Sergei opened his mouth to argue then closed it with a snap when he realized Stuart was right. "I'm sorry, *kotik*. This is not how I wanted the evening to end, but I too want things to be memorable in a good way. I won't walk you to your door, as it will make it harder for me to go if I do." Sergei reached out and pulled Stuart to him for a heated kiss, feeling quite pleased with himself when he pulled back to see the dazed look on Stuart's face. "I'll see you tomorrow night and I'll bring food and a toothbrush."

"Do that." Stuart leaned forward and gave Sergei a quick kiss before letting himself out of the car and making his way to his front door. Sergei watched until a light came on inside before he pulled out of the driveway and headed to the urgent care to meet his family.

Chapter Five

Stuart rearranged the pillows on the couch for the fourth time in the last ten minutes. He didn't know why he was so nervous. They'd had a fantastic evening the night before, outside of the family drama. Their chemistry was certainly off the charts. Sergei had texted him later the previous night to let him know Sasha's arm was indeed broken and that he had a lovely cast to show for it. They had texted each other throughout the day, making plans for dinner. Nothing more was said about the planned activities after the meal.

Stuart had showered and taken care of prep for the evening ahead. He was clean inside and out, as ready as he was going to be. Trimmed and primped. There was nothing to do now but wait. Sergei had texted that he was on his way over fifteen minutes before. He didn't know why he was acting like he was a scared virgin.

Because it has never really meant anything before? It was a means to an end. The scratching of an itch. What if we're horrible in bed? What if we're not? Stuart jumped when the doorbell rang then placed a hand on his chest and took a couple of deep breaths, in through his nose and out through his mouth, to calm his racing heart.

More under control, he walked to the door and pulled it open with a smile on his face, only for the smile to fall when he realized it was his brother. He really needed to check before he opened the door.

"What are you doing here?" Stuart moved to block the door when Andy tried to push past him.

"Can't I come visit my little brother?"

"Nope. It's usually because you want something. I have plans tonight. My date should be here any minute. So, cut to the chase. What do you want?"

"You aren't answering my calls. I've tried calling."

Stuart huffed in exasperation. "I blocked your number after I found out you sold my birthday gift the day after I gave it to you."

"How did yo—?" Andy cut himself off and a calculating look came into his eyes. "Are you stalking me, bro? You do know that my buddy Chris says you have a thing for me."

Stuart gagged. "Hell no. You were my big brother. I looked up to you. You are *so* not my type."

"Oh yeah? What's your type then?" Andy asked with a sneer.

"That would be me." Sergei's growly voice cut into the conversation. "Who are you?" Sergei moved past Andy and stepped in, giving Stuart a peck on the lips before moving to stand beside him, wrapping his arm across his shoulders.

Andy spluttered. "I'm his brother. Who are you?"

"I'm his boyfriend, Sergei Barinov. I have heard a lot about you." Sergei held out his hand to shake and Stuart watched as Andy raised his arm with a bemused look on his face. "Not much of it was good, in case you were wondering."

Andy's gaze shot to Stuart's. "You're dating Sergei Barinov?"

"Yes. He just told you he's my boyfriend." Stuart was surprised when Andy started laughing.

"Oh man, that's rich. You must be amazing in the sack, since there's nothing else exciting about you."

"Thanks a lot. Glad to hear what you really think of me," Stuart said dryly.

"I didn't mean it like that. I mean, look at him, then look at you."

"Not helping, Andy," Stuart got out through gritted teeth. "I'll ask again. What do you want?"

"I need cash."

"I don't have any for you."

"What? You're not even going to ask what I need it for or how much?"

"Nope," Stuart answered, popping the 'p'. "And, as I said, I have plans, so have a great evening." Stuart turned, put his hand on Sergei's chest and pushed him farther into the house so he had room to close the door. He turned to face his brother, pleased to see his shocked look. "Bye now." Stuart closed the door in his face as he started to splutter.

"Hey! Wait! I was still talking to you," Andy shouted from the other side of the closed door, before starting to pound on it.

"Well, I don't have anything to say to you," Stuart shouted back. He turned and grabbed Sergei's hand, leading him into the living room. "So, Sergei, I see no takeout."

"I have ordered dinner to be delivered in a half hour."

"Great. I'm starved. Can I get you something to drink?"

Sergei started chuckling. "Are you going to ignore your brother pounding on the door?"

"Yep. That's the plan. I have nothing to say to him. Drink?"

"Sure. I'll take a beer if you have one."

"I do. Be right back." Stuart went to the kitchen and pulled the refrigerator door open, sticking his head inside to try to cool down. He couldn't believe his brother, asking him for money, thinking he had a crush on him. "As if," Stuart muttered to himself. Stuart grabbed two beers off the shelf and closed the door with his hip before turning to take the bottles back to the living room. He gasped in surprise when he ran into Sergei before he had taken two steps.

"Easy, *kotik*." Sergei brought his hands up to Stuart's upper arms to steady him, then started rubbing his hands up and down in a soothing gesture.

"Sorry. I didn't know you'd followed me."

"I see that."

"Here's your beer. Hope you like it."

"I'm sure I will, but first…" Sergei grabbed the two beer bottles from Stuart's hands and set them on the counter before pulling Stuart into his arms and taking his mouth in a heated kiss.

Stuart moaned then placed his hands on Sergei's waist. He was glad Sergei had had the foresight to put the beer bottles somewhere safe first or he would have dropped them for sure.

Sergei pulled away from the intensity of the kiss, placing gentle pecks on his lips before leaning back to put a little more space between them. "Much as I don't want to stop, dinner should be here any moment. We will revisit this after dinner. *Da*?"

"*Da*," Stuart agreed, making Sergei chuckle, before laying his head on Sergei's shoulder and trying to catch his breath. "By the way, hello. I don't think I ever said that, with the sibling drama that greeted you. How was your day?"

"It was good, *kotik*. And how was yours?"

"Much better now that you're here." Sergei's face creased in a grin.

"I am very happy to hear that. My day is better now too." Stuart slid his hands farther around Sergei's waist and gave him a squeeze in response, loving it when Sergei moved his hands from Stuart's upper arms to wrap his arms around his shoulders and hug him back. They stood there simply holding each other until the sound of the doorbell caused them to break apart.

Sergei gave Stuart a peck on the lips as he stepped back. "That should be dinner. Do you care if I answer the door?"

"Nope. Not a problem. Bring it through to the back patio from the door here." Stuart pointed at the door leading into the backyard that was next to the refrigerator. "It's a beautiful night. I thought we could eat back there."

"Sounds good." Sergei strode toward the front door as Stuart grabbed silverware, napkins and the forgotten beers, took them outside and placed them on the patio table.

Stuart looked around at his outdoor space, quite proud of the oasis he had created. While the yard wasn't very big, he had made use of every inch. A six-foot privacy fence shielded him from view by his neighbors. He had two distinct areas laid out under the covered patio. There was the cooking and eating section, which had his grill and the table and chairs, and at the other side was his lounging section, with a comfortable double chaise longue chair that he often sprawled on at night to relax. The rest of the yard was taken up with flowers and a small swing, just big enough for two. He had placed different solar lights around the edge and had string lights hanging from the rafters of the roof covering the patio. Stuart turned at Sergei's gasp from the doorway.

"This yard is stunning."

Stuart grinned at the man standing with his arms full of food bags. "Thanks. I've worked hard on it."

"It is very you, more so even than the inside that I have seen so far."

"Yeah well, I spend most of my time either in my office, sleeping or here," Stuart answered, spreading his arms to encompass the backyard.

"I can't wait to see the other two spaces then."

Stuart's gaze snapped to Sergei's to find him staring back at him hungrily, and he didn't think it was necessarily for food. "Well, let's eat dinner, then I'll take you for a tour."

"That sounds like an excellent plan. I have had food delivered from the Italian place downtown that you said you liked. We have appetizers and bread then a couple different entrée options. I hope you're hungry."

"Always," Stuart responded with a chuckle. Moving forward, he took one of the bags from Sergei and helped him lay out all the food. "Wow, it looks great. Let's eat." Stuart sat down in one of the chairs and Sergei took the seat next to him. "So, what did you do today, dear?" Stuart asked as he dished out some pasta onto his plate.

Sergei chuckled as he helped himself to some of the food as well. "My day was busy. I had the meeting with the bar owner. He is indeed looking to sell and was very open to my offer. It looks like I will be the owner of Puzzles in a month or so. It was a productive day, all in all."

"Great. How is your brother feeling? I guess I should have asked that first."

"He's fine. He went to school today."

"Really? That seems surprising."

Sergei lifted a shoulder in a half shrug. "Not really. Sasha's pain tolerance is actually pretty high. He's a bit of a klutz and is always hurting himself in one way or another."

"Your mother said something last night about concussions?" Stuart spun his fettucine Alfredo onto his fork as he asked his question, wincing a little when he splattered Alfredo everywhere. Luckily Sergei seemed to be focused on his own food and didn't seem to notice the mess he was making.

"Yeah. He's had two this year, both mild. One more and the doctor said he is going to have to sit out at least six months to give his brain a chance to heal. It's pretty scary, actually."

"Anything to do with the brain is scary. You said he doesn't like playing all that much. Why do your parents still have him do so?"

"All of Sasha's friends are on the team and he's good at the game. Honestly, he is happiest being a bench warmer, though."

Stuart couldn't help his snort of laughter.

"I know, right? My brother doesn't have much of a competitive streak."

"Are you sure he wasn't switched at birth or something? Or did you take all the competitiveness in the gene pool?"

"Ha-ha. You think you are so funny."

Stuart didn't even attempt to hold in his laughter anymore at the affronted look on Sergei's face. Once he was able to stop, Stuart looked at Sergei to find him gazing at him with a mixture of amusement and what appeared suspiciously like fondness.

"What?"

Sergei leaned forward and rubbed his thumb over Stuart's bottom lip. "You seem to have a little bit of Alfredo here and" — he brushed his thumb to wipe at his cheek — "here."

Stuart snatched his napkin off his lap and wiped at his face. "Oops. Sorry about that. You can't take me anywhere."

"Well, it's a good thing we are in the comfort of your home then."

"Yep. A good thing."

"It also means I am free to do this." Sergei put his hand on the back of Stuart's neck and drew him in for a kiss.

"You can do that anytime you want," Stuart said breathlessly when Sergei pulled back a few moments later.

"Good to know, *kotik*. Let us first finish our dinner, then we will explore what else we can do together."

Stuart shot Sergei a grin before focusing back on his food. Anticipation burned low along his nerve endings. It was a pleasant buzz to be enjoyed along with the food, beer and company. Stuart was amazed how easily conversation flowed between the two of them. He had very few people in his life that he felt comfortable enough with to simply talk. Lee was one. Paul was another. Now there was Sergei.

"That was delicious," Stuart said as he finished his last mouthful of food.

"I'm glad you approve. There is dessert as well, but perhaps we can save it for later."

"We are going to have to wait. I am way too full to eat even one more thing. If you want to go relax on the chaise over there" — Stuart indicated with a wave in its direction— "I'll clean up the mess then come join you. Would you like another beer? Or perhaps something else to drink."

"Another beer would be nice. Thank you."

Stuart shot Sergei a quick grin before collecting all the trash and dishes and carrying the first load back inside. He had to make another couple of trips in order to get it all. He had the dessert and leftovers in the refrigerator quickly, though, and grabbed the beers to take with him as he prepared to join Sergei on the large chaise.

Placing the bottles on the table next to the chair, he found Sergei sprawled right in the middle of the lounger. "You're going to have to move to one side or the other if you want me to sit with you."

"Nope." Sergei spread his legs and patted his chest. "I wish for you to sit here in front of me so I can hold you."

"You have some great ideas."

"I have nothing *but* great ideas," Sergei said with mock outrage, making Stuart laugh as he kicked off his sandals and climbed onto the chaise with his back to Sergei's front and leaned against his solid chest. Stuart sighed in contentment when Sergei closed his arms around him. "You are a very easy person to please, *kotik*."

"What makes you say that?"

"Most people I date want to be taken places and to be doing things, where they can show everyone who they are with. The happiest I have seen you is right in this moment."

"I thought we discussed this already. I don't need your money. That's not what a relationship is about to me. It's the time spent together that's important—the conversations and connection."

"I like our connection, *kotik*." Sergei placed a kiss on the side of Stuart's head and tightened his arms around Stuart for a moment before starting to run one hand up and down Stuart's chest and stomach in a lazy caress.

Stuart's cock plumped a little more with every pass, especially when Sergei moved his hand under his T-shirt and started stroking his bare skin. He pressed his chest up into Sergei's hand on the fifth pass over his sensitive nipples. He ached for a harder touch.

"Something you want," Sergei whispered in his ear.

"You. Just you."

"Right answer," Sergei growled before turning Stuart's head with the hand not currently driving him crazy under his shirt and taking his mouth in another of his addictive kisses. After a few moments of the awkward angle, Stuart sat up, turned around and straddled Sergei's lap, unfortunately removing Sergei's hands from his chest while doing so. He quickly stripped off his shirt and gave a quick thought to moving this inside when he felt the slight nip in the air. It was October, after all. The evenings got chilly, even if the daytime hours had been unseasonably warm.

Stuart forgot about the chill when Sergei returned his hands to his body, mapping every inch. Stuart moaned loudly and had to turn his mouth away from Sergei's to gasp for air when Sergei pinched and pulled his left nipple. The twist at the end really wasn't fair. Stuart panted as he moved his hips in a circle, grinding down on the hard bulge he could feel under his ass as Sergei placed his mouth on his right nipple and began to suck. Stuart ground harder and moaned even louder, but he was too turned on to be embarrassed. After a few more grinds, Sergei suddenly grabbed Stuart's hips and halted his movements.

"Let's move this to your bedroom, please. I want our first time to be in a bed."

Stuart took a moment to get his breathing under control. "Yeah, let's do that."

"Not that here doesn't have possibilities, but I would like to make our first memory in your bed."

Stuart nodded as he climbed off Sergei's lap to stand next to the chaise then held out his hand to help him up. Lacing their fingers together, Stuart pulled Sergei after him and through the house to the stairs. Neither of them spoke as they made the trip up the stairs and down the hallway to Stuart's bedroom.

Entering the room, Stuart flipped the switch to turn on the lamps next to his bed. Sergei's gasp next to him brought a smile to Stuart's lips. "You like?"

"I love. It looks so warm and comfortable."

Looking around, Stuart tried to see it as a stranger would. He had chosen rich, warm tones for this room, maroons and grays. It was his sanctuary. There were no television or electronics allowed except his phone. He spent his entire day on his computer. He didn't want to bring it in here. The bed was a four-poster antique, filled with fluffy pillows and soft fabrics. One wall of the room was covered in bookshelves, the shelves bursting with all his favorites, from classics to romance. There were two doors on the opposite wall. One led into the en-suite bathroom and the other into his walk-in closet. He had combined two bedrooms to create the master he'd wanted.

Stuart squeezed Sergei's hand, getting his attention. "You're the first person I've ever brought in here."

"I can see why. This is very personal." Sergei squeezed back. "I am honored to be invited."

Stuart ducked his head, an uncharacteristic shyness taking hold. Sergei used their hand-hold to pull him into his embrace then started backing Stuart toward the bed. "Shall we see what other firsts we can make happen in here?"

"I can definitely get behind that plan." Stuart snaked his arms up and around Sergei's neck and pulled Sergei's mouth to his. He felt the bed against his legs and climbed up onto it without breaking the lip lock, inching backward while pulling Sergei with him until he was lying flat with Sergei sprawled on top of him.

"I think we are perhaps a bit overdressed. Don't you think so, honey?" Stuart gasped as he moved his hands under Sergei's shirt so he could touch the skin on his back.

"Honey?"

Stuart smirked at Sergei. "I'm trying it out. You have a nickname for me. I have to find one for you. Don't like it? How about 'sweetie'?"

"There is nothing sweet about me." Sergei looked almost offended by the idea.

"'Snookums'?"

"Oh, you think you are so funny." Sergei reached out and started tickling Stuart's sides, making him howl with laughter.

"Stop. Stop. No fair."

Stuart looked up after the attack stopped and he got his giggles under control, to find Sergei gazing down on him fondly. "What?"

"I am happy we can be together like this, laughing and having fun as well as the passion. I have not had that before."

"Me either. It's nice."

Sergei leaned down and placed a gentle kiss on Stuart's lips before kissing down his jaw and licking down the side of his neck before blowing on it. The move caused goosebumps to pop up all over Stuart's body and he wiggled underneath Sergei, causing them both to groan before Sergei sat up and removed his shirt, lying back down to press their naked torsos together. Sergei moved his chest slightly side-to-side, the light fur causing wonderful friction on Stuart's very sensitive and very hard nipples.

"I didn't know you had chest hair," Stuart said on a moan.

"Is that a problem?"

"Oh no." Stuart wiggled some more, loving the feel of their bodies rubbing together. "I love that you have hair."

"Good. Good." They spent a few more moments writhing together before Sergei gasped out, "What were we talking about again?"

"Getting naked."

"We were? Oh yeah. Good plan. Let's do that." Sergei shoved backward off Stuart then stepped from the bed to unbuckle his belt and unbutton his pants before shoving them down and off, taking his socks and shoes with them.

Stuart could only lie there and stare as more and more of Sergei's amazing body was revealed. "Wow."

"So you like?" Sergei asked as he flexed a little for Stuart, making his abs ripple.

"I love it. You're amazing. I'm nowhere near as toned."

"I think *you're* amazing and can't wait to see more. Lose the pants, *kotik*."

Stuart moved his hands to the waistband of his pants and unbuttoned and unzipped. Lifting his hips, he shoved his pants and underwear off over the ends of his bare feet then tossed the pants over the side of the bed.

"Beautiful. I am a very lucky man." Sergei climbed back onto the bed and kneeled at his feet, looking him over from head to toe and back again.

Stuart crooked a finger in Sergei's direction. "Come here. I'm feeling a little lonely down here."

Sergei made his way slowly up Stuart's body, stopping at different points to lick, kiss or nibble — a kiss to his left ankle, a lick of his groin while avoiding his straining cock. Stuart's right nipple received a nibble and his left got a lick, causing Stuart to squirm on the bed. Finally, they were face to face and Sergei gazed into Stuart's eyes. "You are gorgeous, *kotik*, and I can't wait to explore every inch of you."

"And I can't wait to explore you, but not tonight. I need." Stuart was only slightly embarrassed by the pleading tone of his voice.

"No. You are right. Not tonight. Tonight, I must be inside you. Do you have supplies?"

Stuart reached under his pillow and pulled out the lube and strip of condoms he had stashed there earlier.

"I do so like a man who is prepared."

"Yeah. Then you should love the surprise I have for you." Stuart gently pushed Sergei to kneel back between his legs so he could pull his legs out and back to expose the end of the black plug he had inserted earlier, in preparation for the night's activities. The hitch of Sergei's breath followed by the deep groan made the hours of anticipation worth it as the plug shifted inside him throughout dinner.

Sergei reached out a hand and traced a trembling finger around the edge of the plug before taking a hold of the handle and giving it a slight tug — not enough to remove it, but enough to make it rub against Stuart's prostate, making him gasp.

"Come on. Please. Don't tease me. I'm on the edge here."

"I see that," Sergei said as he reached out his other hand to run a finger through the stream of precum oozing from Stuart's slit. Raising the finger to his lips, Sergei sucked the finger into his mouth with an audible slurp. Stuart raised his hips in involuntary reaction to the way Sergei looked doing it. Sergei made eye contact with Stuart as he lowered his head to take the crown of Stuart's cock into his mouth, sucking gently as he pulled again on the plug in Stuart's ass.

Stuart felt around on the bed, finding then shoving the strip of condoms at Sergei. "Please. I need you."

"As you wish," Sergei said, coming off the end of Stuart's cock with a pop. Sergei sat up and opened the condom. Stuart salivated as he watched Sergei roll the condom down his member, impressed by its length and girth. Stuart reached for his own cock, only to have

Sergei slap his hand away. "I will give you what you need. Wait."

Stuart grabbed hold of the comforter under him and held on in a desperate effort not to touch himself. He ached. Badly. Finally, Sergei leaned forward and reached for the plug again, pulling it gently from Stuart's body and tossing it to the side of the bed. Sergei lifted Stuart's legs apart and back before placing his hands on the backs of Stuart's thighs, holding him in position as he pressed his cock into Stuart's hungry hole.

Stuart moaned and tightened his legs around Sergei's body as he pressed forward until he felt Sergei's hips against his ass. Stuart had never felt so full or so connected. When he opened his eyes, he found Sergei staring down at him. Stuart crunched up to kiss Sergei's lips. "Move, Barinov."

Sergei moaned and started to work his hips, slowly at first then faster and faster until Stuart was getting the pounding he so needed. Stuart had to reach up to the headboard to brace himself so he didn't hit his head as Sergei's thrusts moved him farther and farther up the bed.

"Please, Sergei. Touch my cock. I need to come."

Sergei released one of Stuart's legs so he could reach between them and wrap a hand around Stuart's cock. He tugged in rhythm to his thrusts, and it only took three yanks before Stuart was coming. He clamped down on Sergei's cock inside him, feeling Sergei come a moment later. The pulses of his release pressed right against his prostate, causing him to spurt more cum on his stomach.

Stuart lay trying to catch his breath for a moment as Sergei gently pulled out and collapsed next to him, resting his head on Stuart's chest. Stuart absently ran his fingers through Sergei's hair, loving its soft texture. After about five minutes of no movement or comment from Sergei, Stuart looked down to realize Sergei had fallen asleep. With a chuckle, Stuart gently rolled Sergei to his back and grabbed some tissues from the bedside table to remove the used condom.

Locating the plug on the bed, Stuart grabbed it too and took both items to the bathroom. Stuart wet a washcloth and wiped himself off. Using the toy cleaner on the counter, Stuart cleaned the plug and left it on a towel to air dry before wetting another cloth to take back to his sleeping lover and wipe him down.

Sergei grumbled in his sleep but didn't awaken, even as Stuart maneuvered the comforter out from under him and pulled it up to cover him. Stuart took a moment to pick up Sergei's clothes from the floor and lay them out on the chair in the corner of the room that he used for reading and line his shoes up underneath before switching off the light and climbing into bed with Sergei. Stuart couldn't help smiling when Sergei reached for him in his sleep and pulled him so he was again lying with his head on Stuart's chest. Stuart went back to running his fingers through Sergei's hair, letting the motion and the warmth of the body snuggled into him lull him to sleep.

Chapter Six

Sergei woke slowly, enjoying the feel of the warm body under his. He inhaled Stuart's unique scent. It was vanilla, combined with an underlying musk that was all Stuart. He listened to Stuart's steady heartbeat under his ear for a few more minutes before his bladder forced him to get up and head to the bathroom. Once those needs were taken care of, he washed and dried his hands before glancing at his watch. He was shocked to realize he'd been asleep for a couple of hours. There was something soothing about being with Stuart. The man seemed to calm the restlessness in his soul. He hoped Stuart was ready, because now that he had confirmation they were as compatible in bed as they were out of it, he wasn't planning to let him go any time soon…if ever.

Sergei stood in the bathroom doorway watching Stuart sleep for a few moments in the light from the bathroom before looking around for his clothes, finally spying them on the very comfortable-looking chair in the corner. He grabbed his boxer briefs and threw them on before heading to the kitchen to get the dessert he had picked up to go with dinner. Finding a tray on top of the refrigerator, Sergei loaded it with the dessert, forks, napkins and a couple of bottles of water and carried it all back upstairs to see if Stuart was awake yet.

"You're still here." Stuart's voice in the semi-darkness startled Sergei a little.

"Where else would I be? We're having a sleepover, are we not?" Sergei used his elbow to switch on the light before making his way to the bed and placing the tray next to Stuart in the middle.

Stuart was adorably sleep-tousled, and he really shouldn't be charmed by the worried furrow of his brow. "Well, yeah, but you weren't here when I woke up."

"I'd never simply leave without telling you. I thought we could enjoy this wonderful dessert that I brought in bed."

The furrow disappeared and Stuart gave him a smile that Sergei had to taste. Leaning down, he placed a gentle kiss on Stuart's lips, pulling away before it turned into anything more. After moving around to the other side of the bed, he climbed in and leaned against the headboard as Stuart scooted up to do the same.

Stuart straightened the sheet over his legs while looking at the different sweets that Sergei had displayed on the tray. "We seem to spend a lot of time eating together. Maybe we should plan to do something more active on our next date. At this rate, we're going to end up each weighing six hundred pounds."

"I don't think that's going to be a problem, especially if we continue to burn off calories as we did earlier."

Sergei gave a Stuart a smirk and a wink as he said it, fascinated to see a blush rise from about midway down Stuart's chest and slowly move up to his face. He chuckled before taking pity on him and changing the subject. "What type of more active things would you like to do? I like to hike around the parks."

"That could be fun to do together. I like to hike too. It helps me stay in shape. I spend a lot of time sitting at my desk. I have gym equipment in one of the spare bedrooms that I try to use at least every other day too."

"How many bedrooms do you have?"

"Well, I combined two to make this larger master. There are two more up here. One is my home gym and one is going to be a guest room, but I haven't done anything with it or the guest bathroom yet. They're bad."

"Surely they can't be *that* bad." Sergei took a bite of cake as he waited for a response from Stuart.

"They are, but they haven't been a priority."

After swallowing the delicious cake, Sergei continued his line of questioning. "Your office is on the first floor then?"

"Yep. My office is actually in the room that is supposed to be the dining room. As it's just me, there was no need for me to have a separate room for eating. The eat-in kitchen and breakfast bar work fine. Those two rooms, the living room and a powder room are all down there."

"I can't wait to see it, including the hideous guest bathroom."

"Okay. Don't say I didn't warn you. These desserts are delicious, but I can't eat any more. I swear I'm still full from dinner. Come on. Let me put some clothes on and I'll give you the grand tour."

"You don't have to get dressed on my account. I'm enjoying the view."

"Yeah? Well, some of my window shades are open downstairs. You'd be sharing the view with the neighbors."

"Then you definitely need to put something on. I don't share."

Stuart chuckled as he climbed out of bed and grabbed his boxer briefs and a pair of shorts from his dresser drawers. "Got it. No sharing. Have you seen the master bath?"

"Yes. It's quite nice. You did a good job."

"Lee helped. He had some experience from redoing the bathroom at his old apartment. Luckily, even my guest bathroom is not quite as bad as what Lee had to deal with there."

"I saw the before and after pictures. Lee does amazing work."

"He really does. Everything he touches turns out great. Your car is a prime example."

Sergei followed Stuart out of the room, pausing when Stuart stopped at the first bedroom to flip on the light switch. Stuart went on to the next room and flipped on that light too, as Sergei peeked into the room and saw the very nicely appointed gym Stuart had set up.

"Wow. You've got everything you need for a great workout—free weights, a bench, a treadmill and an entire weight-lifting system. I've seen actual gyms with less equipment."

"I know, right? I don't like working out in front of people, though, so I've been buying gear piece by piece."

"Why don't you like working out in front of people?"

"Well, I wasn't exactly skinny growing up. I was the geeky, overweight computer guy. I was short too. I didn't hit my growth spurt until college. The only thing I was missing was the glasses. Luckily, I did and do have good vision. When I first decided to start working out, I wasn't comfortable enough to do it in front of people. I did a ton of research and bought a couple of things, then I added a few more…then a few more. My uncle had a basement in his house where I kept it all." After looking around for a moment, Stuart continued, "I may have overdone it, but I do use everything."

"Well, the results are certainly there. I never would have guessed you used to be overweight in any way."

"Yeah. I've worked hard. You're welcome to use any of the equipment anytime. Come on. Let me show you the rest."

Stuart pointed to the next room down the hall. Sergei had been warned but was still shocked at the state of it, after seeing the rest of the house. The room was very dark. It looked like graffiti was spray-painted on one of the walls, while the other three walls were painted completely black. There was a hideous beige carpet on the floor, stained in multiple locations with who knew what. One spot looked suspiciously like blood.

"What happened here?"

Stuart laughed. "This was, and still is, the worst room in the house. The house was a student rental before I bought it. The previous occupant of this room had their own unique decorating style. I keep going back and forth to decide between ripping out and replacing all the drywall or trying to paint over it. I think it would probably take less time to rip it all out.

I'm hoping to find hardwood under the carpet, but I'm scared to touch the carpet to rip it out and check."

"I would suggest investing in a hazmat suit before touching that. That's a lot of black paint on the walls. Is the graffiti supposed to be something?" Sergei cocked his head, first one way then the other, trying to make sense of all the squiggly lines and blotches of different colored paints.

"Not that I can tell. I tried to find some meaning in the mess, but I think it's just chaos. I'm really hoping it isn't a reflection of the previous occupant's mind."

Sergei nodded. "I truly hope not. That would be bad."

"That would be *very* bad," Stuart agreed with a chuckle. "Come on. There is just one more horrible room then the rest is nice. I promise."

Sergei left the room with one more glance back at the graffiti mess before heading toward the hall bathroom. "This isn't as bad as I was thinking it was going to be."

"Nah. It's just really tired and needs new everything. I'm thinking I'm going to get a dumpster, rip out the drywall and carpeting in the other room and gut everything out of here and be done with it. Then I can start fresh."

"Good plan. What is next on the tour?"

"That's it for the upstairs. Come on. I'll show you my lair downstairs."

"Ah. And do you use the powers of your lair for good or evil?"

"I try to stay on the side of good. Sometimes it's hard, though."

A wave of sadness crossed Stuart's face.

"What's that look for?"

"My mom's church contacted me about making a website for them, at my mother's recommendation. They aren't necessarily anti-gay, but they aren't exactly welcoming either. If they'd contacted me directly, I'm not sure I would have agreed, but they used the mom card."

"The mom card is hard to go up against, especially when they don't use it very often."

"I know, right? I couldn't say no. Religion isn't my thing, though, so it's hard."

"Sadly, anyone who is in business must, from time to time, do things they don't like. It's the price of doing business. The trick is to pick your battles."

As they were talking, they'd been making their way downstairs and down the hall, passing first the standard powder room, which was painted a soothing blue color, then on to the office. Sergei was both excited and nervous about seeing the office. He had a feeling it would show Stuart's true personality. Walking through the door, Sergei couldn't hold back his gasp.

"This is amazing."

Stuart stood with his hands in the pockets of his shorts, looking so epically, nervously adorable that Sergei just wanted to wrap him up in a hug, so he did, taking the few steps to be in front of Stuart before yanking him into his arms. Stuart wrapped his arms around Sergei's waist and tentatively returned it.

"What's this hug for?" Stuart asked.

"Isn't that one of the benefits of having a boyfriend? To be able to hold them whenever you want?"

"I guess," Stuart answered hesitantly. "But the hug was very random."

"You looked nervous about showing me all this." Moving to Stuart's side, still keeping one arm wrapped around his waist, Sergei waved his other arm to encompass the room. "Your office is amazing. It's like a command room."

"That's kind of how I think of it. With multiple monitors, I can keep track of different things. I'm usually working on one computer while I run diagnostics or whatever on at least one other, which is why I have three different computers and monitors."

"What about all this?" Sergei asked as he pointed at the wall covered in superhero paraphernalia.

"I like superheroes. I told you I was a geek. I usually go to the comic conventions downtown. If you wear a costume, no one knows who you are, and it's very relaxing."

"Yes. My little brother and his friends also go to these conventions. Their dream is to go to the one in Los Angeles. "

"Yeah, that would be amazing, but we do get a lot of great stars who do the ones in Raleigh as well."

"Do you have a lot of costumes?" Sergei was surprised when this brought a bit of a blush to Stuart's cheeks.

"Yeah. Quite a few. They take up space in my walk-in in the master. Once I have the spare room done, the plan is to move them in there."

"Well, you and my brother should have plenty to chat about at Sunday dinner then. I often don't know what he's talking about."

Stuart chuckled. "Yeah. Speaking geek is an acquired skillset and takes dedication. You were serious about me going to Sunday dinner?"

"I never joke about Sunday dinner. Mama invited you herself. She wishes to meet you."

"Okay. Well, I wanted to make sure you wanted me to go. I could come up with an excuse if you weren't ready to introduce us."

"I'm ready to introduce you. In fact, I can't wait to introduce you. Okay?" Once Sergei received Stuart's nod of acceptance, he looked around the room again. "Why do you have a recliner in here?"

"When I need a break, I sometimes sit in the chair and read either manga or comics—or sometimes something else like a manual or computer book. Usually it's manga or comics, though. It gives me a reset opportunity, especially if I'm stuck on something."

"Ah. That makes sense."

A look Sergei decided to label as shy crossed Stuart's face. "You're welcome to come join me here in my office anytime. The chair really is quite comfy."

"And are there a lot of people who have this invitation? Or am I special?"

"Only two. You and Lee. Sometimes Lee comes to hang out when he wants a quiet place to sketch."

"You and Lee have gotten pretty tight over the last year, haven't you?"

"Yeah. It's nice. I don't have to impress Lee and he doesn't have to impress me. We can just be when we're together."

"It's nice to have a friend like that. I hope I'll be one of those friends for you too."

Stuart gave a surprised snort. "Yeah, well, our chemistry is off the charts, so I don't see me being one hundred percent comfortable around you anytime soon. I'm very comfortable with you as a person already and that scares me a little."

"Why does it scare you?"

"Because I keep waiting for you to realize you can do so much better than me."

"We really have to work on your self-confidence, *kotik*. One day you will see yourself the way I do. You are amazingly sexy, warm and intelligent, and I can't wait to learn everything about you. Now what do you say that we take this discussion back to bed? I have much to learn about you." Bending, Sergei gave Stuart a bone-melting kiss before taking his hand and leading him out of the room. "Including how well you top."

"You'd let me?"

"Of course."

Sergei laughed when Stuart suddenly moved ahead of him and began pulling him out of the door and toward the stairs.

Chapter Seven

Stuart wiped his sweaty hands on his jeans after he'd closed the passenger-side car door. He was meeting Sergei's parents. He'd never met parents before. This was a big deal, especially meeting Sergei's mother, who his boyfriend worshipped. He already had strikes against him with Natasha.

Stuart pulled open the rear passenger door and grabbed the two bunches of flowers he had purchased for the women of the family. He shot Sergei a dirty look when he heard him chuckling.

"Relax, *kotik*. They're not going to bite. They will love you."

"It's easy for you to say for me to relax. You don't have to worry about disapproving family members, since the only family I have isn't really part of my life."

"Oh? And what would you call Mama V, the woman who, while standing on the sideline of a children's soccer game, threatened me with bodily harm if I hurt you? I dare you to tell her she isn't family."

Stuart couldn't help the huge smile on his face. "I didn't know she was going to do that. I was as surprised as you were. You didn't have to go with me to the game, you know."

"I know. I wasn't quite ready to let you out of my sight yet that morning. It was fun. Sam turned into quite the competitor when she got on the field. It was very surprising to witness. She's usually so quiet, compared to Claire."

"I know, right? I'm always shocked. It's great to see, though."

"It really is. Now come, *kotik*. No more stalling. Let's go in."

Sergei placed a hand on Stuart's back and gently guided him into the house. He didn't bother to ring the bell. He simply let himself in with a key. "Mama! We're here."

Sergei's mother's heavily accented voice called out from a room to the right. "We're all in the kitchen. Come on through."

Sergei steered Stuart in the direction of the voice, leading him down the hallway a little bit then into the door on the right, which led into a huge, open kitchen, eating area and a large living space with a wall of windows looking out onto the back yard. Everything was shining stainless steel and granite and about three times the size of Stuart's kitchen. It was also full of people. Stuart started to take a step back as everyone turned to look at the two of them when they walked through the door but found his way blocked by Sergei's presence behind him.

An older woman who looked like a feminine and much smaller version of Sergei moved around the counter and came up to Stuart. "Are those for me? You should not have."

"Yes, ma'am. Well, one is for you. One is for Natasha."

As Stuart said her name, a blonde head spun his way from where Sergei's sister was perched on a stool at the breakfast bar, studiously ignoring them after the initial look. Stuart saw the surprised pleasure in her eyes before she adopted a bored expression. Stuart handed one set of flowers to Sergei's mother then awkwardly tried to mimic her as she kissed both his cheeks.

"I will put these in water. Natasha, come get your flowers and thank Stuart for thinking of you." The stern tone of voice was in direct contrast with the sweet woman who had thanked Stuart, and it made him jump. He could certainly see why Sergei's mother terrified him.

Natasha did as she was told, albeit reluctantly and through gritted teeth. "Thank you for thinking of me and bringing me flowers."

"Be nice, Natasha," Sergei growled at her from his spot behind Stuart.

"I *am* being nice." Natasha took the bouquet and flounced her way over to the sink, where her mother had produced a couple of vases.

"I never understood the word 'flounced' before now," Stuart turned his head and whispered to Sergei. "That was impressive."

Sergei chuckled in Stuart's ear, making him shiver. "Yes. My sister has dramatic down to a science." Louder, he said, "Now come on. Let me introduce you to everyone else. They're all excited to meet you. First, here is Natasha's boyfriend Reggie. They're students together at college."

The young man barely looked up from his phone, where he was playing some kind of game, to give a "Hey," before looking back down at his phone again.

"Hey. Nice to meet you."

Reggie grunted in response.

"Moving on. This is my cousin Nikolai. He's the son of my mother's younger brother. We've always been close. I have a few more cousins around of some of my mother's other siblings, but I don't have a lot to do with them."

Stuart stuck his hand out to shake with the young man, who was exactly as Sergei had described him. In direct contrast to Sergei, Nikolai was very slight. He couldn't be more than one hundred forty pounds soaking wet and stood about five feet seven. While Sergei was the epitome of tall, dark and handsome, Nikolai was blue-eyed and blond-haired with a streak of pink through it. He was amazingly striking in his own right. As opposed to Sergei's tailored look, Nikolai was currently wearing a Cher T-shirt and a pair of shorts, with flip-flops on his feet and some kind of shiny gloss on his lips. "Pleased to meet you, Nikolai. Sergei says you're a financial wizard."

"Wizard in training, actually, if you want to be technical about it, but yes. Pleased to meet you as well. I've heard a lot about you from Sergei."

"Really?" Stuart didn't know why that surprised him, but it did.

"Yep. I was beginning to think you were a figment of his imagination. He's talked about you since Kirk and Eric's wedding, kicking himself for not getting your number or at least your last name so he could've found your number. The whining was quite annoying."

"I do *not* whine. Don't tell tales, Nikolai."

"Yes, Sergei." Once Sergei turned his head to answer a question put to him by his mother, Nikolai mouthed, "He *so* whined." Stuart couldn't help his snort of laughter. He had a feeling he and Nikolai were going to get along great.

"I don't know what was said, but I do believe it is time to keep moving." Sergei led Stuart over to the living room where the two males of the family had relocated while Stuart had been talking to Nikolai. They were currently sitting on the couch watching a soccer game. "Stuart, this is my father Sean Hamilton and next to him is my brother Alexander, but we all call him Sasha."

"Pleased to meet you, sir." Stuart stuck out his hand as the older gentleman stood up and surprised him by pulling him into a hug instead of taking the proffered hand.

"None of that 'sir' crap. Call me Sean. We're not that formal around here. We leave that to Sergei. Welcome. Come have a seat. Do you like soccer?" Sean pulled Stuart down with him as he sat back on the couch.

"I watch it occasionally." Stuart looked around Sean so he could see Sasha. "How are you feeling, Sasha?"

"I'm good. It sucks to have a cast, but at least it's not my writing hand."

"Well, that's one good thing. Your brother was quite worried about you."

Sasha rolled his eyes. "Sergei is a worrywart. Whatever he does, he does wholeheartedly."

Stuart again couldn't hold back his chuckle. "That seems to be a pretty accurate description." Stuart shot a glance in Sergei's direction to find him standing with his arms crossed, looking militant.

"What is this? Pick on Sergei day?"

"Yep," Sasha snarked back. "There will be a parade later and everything."

"Brat." Sergei plopped down on the couch next to Sasha and pulled him into a headlock. Sergei used his other hand to mess up Sasha's hair.

Sasha chuckled and shoved Sergei away. "Stop messing up my hair."

Stuart watched with amusement to see this new side of Sergei. It was definitely different from the persona he adopted out in the world and was even different from the relaxed version he was with him behind closed doors. This was Sergei in family mode. Stuart was beginning to realize that Sergei was a bit of a chameleon when it came to his relationships.

He turned to watch the soccer game with Sean while half listening to Sergei and Sasha's discussion of Sasha's classes. He paid a little closer attention when the subject switched to the play Sasha was auditioning for at a local theater company.

"I know the director there. She and I went to the same college and did some theater classes and productions together."

Sasha's eyes got big. "You did theater?"

"Yes. Why does that surprise you?"

"You look more like a football player."

Stuart grimaced. "Yeah, well, I didn't hit my growth spurt until college. I was five feet five inches tall until after my eighteenth birthday."

"Really?" The look of shock and incredulity on Sasha's face was amusing. Stuart couldn't hold back his chuckle.

"Yep. I was one hundred percent nerd. I still am, if I'm honest. I just hide it a little better, is all."

"Tell him about your collections and costumes," Sergei added as he removed the arm he had thrown across Sasha's shoulders and leaned back into the couch cushions. Sasha twisted sideways to be able to look directly at Stuart, pulling his right leg up in front of him and leaning back against Sergei's shoulder for support.

"You have costumes?"

"I do. I like to dress up for the conventions in town. It's a lot of fun. I also have a large manga and comic book collection that you're welcome to look at and read anytime."

"Wow. I can't wait to see it." Sasha was almost vibrating in his excitement.

Nikolai made his way into the living room and sprawled in one of the armchairs, draping his legs over one arm and leaning his shoulders into the opposite corner of the chair. "What's got Sasha so excited?"

"Stuart cosplays, and he has comics and manga and he did some theater in college."

"Re-a-lly?" Nikolai dragged out the word into three syllables, raising an eyebrow in disbelief. "You don't look the type."

Stuart laughed. "Is there a type? I mean, Stallone has a Bachelor's of Fine Arts from the University of Miami, for goodness sake."

Nikolai's laughter was a little trill of sound, making Stuart smile. "That is true. I guess that I, of all people, shouldn't stereotype."

Turning back to Sasha, Stuart asked, "When are auditions?"

"Next week. We're doing *Into the Woods*."

"Oh, that's a fun one. What role are you trying for?"

"I'd like to play one of the princes. There are a couple of guys who are really, really good, who will probably get the baker and Jack." Sasha shrugged. "All I can do is try, right?"

Stuart gave him a smile. "Right. Maybe I can hear your audition material after dinner. How would that be?"

"That'd be great. Thank you."

"Dinner is ready, everyone," Sergei's mother called from the kitchen. "Come eat."

Sergei's father paused the game on the television and they all went to the table.

"Come sit next to me, *kotik.*"

"But that's my seat," Natasha whined and threw Stuart a dirty look.

"Here, Stuart," Sasha offered. "You can have my seat. It's on the other side of Sergei, so we don't have to listen to Natasha whine all through dinner. I'll sit next to Nikolai."

Stuart said, "Thank you, Sasha."

At the same time, Natasha said, "I don't whine."

"Children, don't argue." Daria interrupted before the argument could escalate. "Let's just sit and have a nice family dinner."

"Yes, Mama." The chorus of voices all speaking at once made Stuart jump. He hustled to take his seat next to Sergei as everyone rushed to their spots at the table. A delicious-looking lasagna was placed in the center. There were also side dishes, including salad and bread and some vegetables. Stuart filled his plate as items were passed around.

"This is delicious, ma'am," Stuart addressed Sergei's mother.

"Please call me Daria. None of this 'ma'am'. I already feel old enough."

"Yes, ma'am. I mean…Daria."

"I am glad you like the food. Next weekend is Sean's turn to cook. He will be making barbecue ribs. You will come again. *Da*?"

"Yes, ma'am. I mean…Daria."

"Good. You will not be a stranger. Now eat."

Stuart ate while enjoying the conversation and the feeling of being with a family again. He sat back with a groan after eating his fill and then some.

"You like my mama's cooking?"

"It's incredible. Remind me to work out before we come next Sunday. I need to do something to counteract all this."

"I will." Sergei leaned over and kissed the side of Stuart's head before turning back to his food.

Stuart looked up to find Nikolai staring at them in astonishment. "What?"

"I've never seen him be casually affectionate with anyone but family before. He's always been formal, even with those he dates. It's nice to see."

Sergei pointed his fork at Nikolai. "Stop scaring him."

"How am I scaring him?" Nikolai's tone was incredulous.

"By staring at him like he is an animal in the zoo."

"Well, I have heard you call him *kotik*…"

"Ugh. Will you two stop talking about me like I'm not right here?" Stuart finally had to interject.

"Don't mind them," Daria said from her spot at one end of the table. "They have always spoken so to each other. It does not matter the topic. They will find a way to make it a discussion. Ignore them. Now, tell me about you, Stuart."

Stuart felt a moment of panic until Sergei reached under the table and squeezed his knee in support. Stuart put his hand under the table and clasped Sergei's hand in response, shooting him a quick glance before focusing his attention on Sergei's mother, all sixty terrifying inches of her. Stuart swallowed hard.

"I'm not sure what you want to know. I own my own web design and graphic arts business. I don't make as much as Sergei here, but I make enough to meet my needs and set some aside for a rainy day. We share some of the same friends. They're really more of a family than friends at this point."

"And what of your biological family?"

"Mama," Sergei interrupted, "perhaps this isn't dinner-time conversation. Let's just enjoy this wonderful meal you prepared."

"What did I say?" Daria asked, looking confused.

"It's okay, Sergei." Stuart squeezed the hand he still held under the table. "I don't have much to do with my biological family, ma'am. My father died when I was young. It was just me and my Mom until she remarried. I was asked to leave my stepfather's house when I turned eighteen. I was lucky enough to be able to live with my biological father's brother when I wasn't at college. Unfortunately, he passed away. I speak to my mother once a month or so, but she's busy with my stepfather and her church. It's all good. I have my friends, including my roommate from college — and now Sergei."

"Did you get thrown out because you're a faggot?" Reggie asked with a sneer.

"Reginald," Daria barked, "we do *not* use such language in this house."

"What?" Natasha inquired with an innocent expression belied by the glee in her eyes. "It's a fair question."

"Natasha!" Daria followed the name with a spew of Russian that Stuart didn't understand, but the tone and Natasha's belligerent expression said it wasn't anything good.

Suddenly Natasha stood up and, with a hair toss, started to flounce away from the table. "Come on, Reggie. We're out of here. I'm not really hungry anymore anyway."

Reggie hurriedly took one more bite of the food on his plate before getting up to follow Natasha out of the room. "Thanks for dinner. It was really good. Sorry about the faggot thing." With a wave, he was gone.

"I'm supposed to be the drama queen in this family," Nikolai said with a pout.

Everyone laughed, as was clearly Nikolai's intention, lowering the tension at the table significantly.

"I apologize for Natasha and her boyfriend. I do not know what is going on with that girl lately." Daria cast a concerned look at the doorway where Natasha had exited so dramatically. "I am sorry you do not have much family, but you have us now."

"Which is both a good and bad thing, as you've seen," Sean added with a chuckle.

Stuart realized he was clutching way too hard at Sergei's hand and loosened his grip as he took a few deep breaths. "I'm sorry that I've upset Natasha."

Sean held up his hand to halt Stuart's words. "This isn't really about you. There's been something going on with her for a while now. As we told Sergei the other day, she's become a bit of a brat. You just happen to be her latest target. She needs to learn to share Sergei. She's never had to do that, so it's a shock for her."

"I've spoiled her by always answering whenever she calls. She's used to having my attention whenever she wants it, but that's no excuse for the way she's treating you. I'll talk to her."

"No, you will not," Daria told Sergei forcefully. "You will live your life. The world does not revolve around your sister, no matter what she thinks. You will stop catering to her every whim. Understood?"

"*Da*, Mama."

"*Spasibo*." She turned back to Stuart. "I apologize for the bad manners of my daughter and her boyfriend. I am, however, curious. Did your family throw you away because you were gay?"

"No, ma'am. It was more because I was another man's son."

"Oh," Daria raised her hand to her mouth in shock.

"Yes, Mama. I know that I was really lucky that you met Sean." Leaning around Stuart, Sergei pinned Sean with a look. "I don't think I've ever really said thank you. Thank you for taking me as your son when you took Mama as your wife."

Stuart watched as Sean's eyes filled before he stood to walk around the table. Sergei got up to meet him and they embraced.

"Oh. Group hug," Nikolai shouted before jumping up, running around the table and embracing the two men.

"Nikolai!" Sergei stepped back and wiped his eyes and shook his head at Nikolai's antics.

Stuart was trying hard not to laugh but lost the battle when he made eye contact with Sasha. Suddenly, everyone was laughing, making it hard for Stuart to stop. He looked up and found Daria gazing at him with fondness.

"I have a feeling you are going to be very good for this family, Stuart. Now everyone, let's finish eating."

The rest of the meal was filled with great conversation and food and laughter. It was a true family meal. Stuart fit in so easily—and that scared him.

Chapter Eight

Sergei rang the doorbell at Stuart's house, dressed in costume for the Halloween party they were getting ready to attend at Puzzles with all the guys. He would be completing the sale of the bar on the Monday after the huge annual Halloween party. Traditionally, the bar made a fantastic profit on the event and it was one of the conditions of the sale. The previous owner didn't want to close before reaping the rewards of that particular event. Sergei couldn't exactly blame him. Puzzles was going to be a great addition to his real estate portfolio.

Sergei's thoughts were interrupted by the door opening in front of him. Whatever he was going to say was forgotten as he got a look at Stuart's costume. He barked out a laugh. Stuart was dressed in a Tigger onesie, complete with hood and ears.

"What?" Stuart asked with a smirk. "You always call me kitten. I thought you would like it."

"I love it actually. It's just not what I was expecting."

"And what, pray tell, were you expecting?" Stuart asked with a knowing grin.

"I was kind of expecting something a little sexier, but knowing how reserved you are, I'm not sure why I thought that."

Stuart laughed out loud at Sergei's pout, obviously not affected by it at all. "Yeah. You really should have known better. Where's your costume, anyway? I thought we agreed to dress up. You're just wearing your normal suit."

Sergei chuckled and removed his tie then slowly unbuttoned his dress shirt to reveal the Superman T-shirt underneath, before taking a pair of black-framed glasses out of his shirt pocket and placing them on his face.

"That is *so* cheating!"

"What's cheating about it?"

"Oh, you're in so much trouble, mister." Stuart grabbed something from behind him and whapped Sergei with it. Glancing down, Sergei was amused to realize it was the tail of Stuart's costume. "Next year we'll have to pick out costumes together."

A thrill went through Sergei, and he grabbed hold of Stuart and yanked him into a heated kiss.

"Not that I'm complaining," Stuart asked breathlessly long moments later, "but what was that for?"

"That was for acknowledging that we'll be together next year to pick out costumes together."

"Oh. Yeah. I guess I did, didn't I?"

"Yep. And you didn't even qualify it with an 'if'. That makes me so happy." Sergei leaned down and gave Stuart another steamy kiss. "You know, we could stay here tonight. I doubt anyone would even miss us."

Stuart's phone dinged with an incoming text and he glanced down at it, clutched in his hand, then turned it around to show to Sergei. On it was a text from Lee.

We know Sergei just got back from his weeklong business trip, but don't even think of blowing us off. We will come and get you if you don't show up.

It was ended with a devil emoji.

Sergei sighed. "I guess we've been told. Come on. Let's get going. The sooner we go, the sooner we can come back and get reacquainted." He waggled his eyebrows up and down and leered at his boyfriend before roping an arm around his waist and yanking him in for another kiss. "I missed you."

"I've missed you too. I'm glad you made it back in time. How was New York?"

"Windy and cold. They're expecting snow." Sergei shuddered. "It's only October."

"Yeah. There's a reason I live in Raleigh, not including the fact that I was born here. I don't like to be cold, but I like the seasons. The few really cold days we have are enough for me."

"I got enough cold in Russia. I don't like it either."

Stuart's phone dinged with another text.

Are you on your way yet?

Sergei laughed and reluctantly let Stuart go. "We'd better get going."

"Oh, here." Stuart stopped typing his reply to reach toward the table next to the door and grab a key, his phone and his wallet. "This is for you," Stuart said as he handed Sergei the key. The confusion must have shown on Sergei's face, because Stuart continued. "It's a key to my place. I thought it'd make things easier."

Sergei tried to make eye contact with Stuart, but Stuart ducked under his arm and walked out of the door. "Never mind the fact that I don't have any pockets, so nowhere to put my keys, phone and wallet tonight. I was hoping you could hold my wallet and phone for me." Stuart looked over his shoulder at Sergei as he made his way to the car.

"Thank you for the key, *kotik*. I'm honored to have it. I'll get you a key to my place as well."

"Oh no. That's not why I—"

"I know it's not, but you'll get a key, nevertheless. I am curious, though. Why don't you put your wallet in the pocket of your clothes underneath?"

"Who said I'm wearing anything underneath?" Stuart asked with a smirk and a wink before he climbed into the passenger side of the car and closed the door behind him.

Sergei stumbled as the possibilities ran through his mind then rushed to get into the other side of the car. He turned in his seat to look at Stuart and found him laughing. "You *are* wearing something under your costume, aren't you?"

"Does a jock strap count?"

"Get out of the car."

"Why? We need to go. We're going to be late."

"The party is all night."

"Yeah, but we're meeting everyone for dinner first. Let's go, Barinov. We have reservations."

"You will not leave my side tonight, *kotik*."

Stuart laughed at Sergei after that statement. "I wasn't planning to."

"Good."

Sergei spent the drive to Puzzles trying to get his raging libido under control. His horny condition was not helped when Stuart put his hand on Sergei's thigh and started to run it up and down his inseam. Sergei grabbed it to stop the movement then raised it to his mouth to place a kiss on the back before lacing their fingers together and moving their entwined hands to rest on top of the car's middle console. "If you wish to go to this party, you need to keep your hands to yourself."

He was answered by another chuckle from Stuart. "Yes, dear."

"Smartass."

"Yep, but I'm *your* smartass."

Sergei shot Stuart a look to find him eying him with amusement. Sergei gave Stuart's hand a squeeze. "Actually, all of you is mine, not just your ass."

"So funny. Way to ruin the moment, dickhead."

"I am simply stating a fact, *kotik*. You're mine."

"True, but you're also mine."

"It is good that you understand that."

They pulled up to the restaurant and into the already-crowded lot. There weren't many spots left, but they were lucky enough to get a decent one before they exited the car and headed to the entrance. Stuart pulled his hood back up as they approached the door.

"Ready, babe?"

"Babe?"

"I'm still trying out endearments for you."

"I like 'babe'." Sergei reached out and opened the door, holding it for Stuart to go inside first.

"Well, good. We have a winner then."

Sergei leaned down and snagged a kiss as Stuart went past him. "We have a winner indeed." Sergei hoped Stuart knew he wasn't just talking about the endearment.

After following his boyfriend inside, Sergei snagged Stuart's hand again and twined their fingers together before leading him into the restaurant. He saw Lee first, mainly because he was standing up and waving at them to get their attention, but also partly because he was wearing a Robin costume, complete with green tights and a yellow cape. They made their way to the corner where tables had been pushed together to accommodate their large group.

Sergei acknowledged the hellos from everyone and made his way to the two empty seats next to Lee. Looking around the table, he wasn't surprised to see that Saul was dressed as Batman, Kirk was dressed as Buzz Lightyear, while Eric was dressed as Woody. Sergei could only shake his head at Nikolai, who was dressed as Little Red Riding Hood. Nikolai gave him a wink with one of his false-eye-lashed lids. "Nikolai, your make-up is flawless, as usual."

"Thank you, darling."

One of Lee and Kirk's co-workers was there in a mechanics' overall. "Will, you dressed as a mechanic for Halloween? You *are* a mechanic."

"I know. That's why it's perfect. I didn't have to spend any extra money on a costume."

Everyone laughed as Will raised a finger and tapped it to his temple.

"Very thrifty indeed," Stuart answered.

"So, what do you think of Stuart's costume?" Lee asked Sergei with a knowing smirk.

"The costume itself is great."

"Why did you say it that way?" Saul asked from the other side of Lee.

Stuart chuckled as he answered. "The costume is warm. Sergei's struggling with what I'm wearing *under* the costume — or not wearing, to be more accurate." Stuart waited until everyone finished laughing to continue. "Sergei has my wallet and keys since I don't have anywhere to put them."

"Yeah. I would have the same problem if not for my trusty utility belt," Lee said. More laughter.

Dinner was interrupted a few minutes later by the arrival of Natasha at their table.

"What are *you* doing here?" Natasha asked without bothering to greet anyone.

"Don't be rude, Natasha. Say hello to my friends."

"You can't be here," Natasha grumbled, ignoring Sergei's comment.

"And why not? It *is* a free country after all, plus I will own this place come Monday. I wanted to get a feel for how the Halloween party goes."

A look of horror crossed Natasha's face. "Are you going to turn it into a gay bar? My friends and I like this place."

"No, Natasha," Sergei snapped, "I'm not going to turn this place into a gay bar, although you have no say as to what I do with it. It will be a bar where people can be themselves, however. Welcoming to *all*. Now, I don't know where this attitude has come from, but I don't like it. Go join your friends and let me enjoy mine."

Sergei startled when Stuart gripped his thigh under the table. Tearing his gaze away from where he was watching Natasha storm away, he looked first at Stuart then at all his friends before taking a breath to try to relax. "I apologize for my sister's rudeness. I have no idea what has gotten into her lately. She used to be so sweet."

Nikolai scoffed then responded when Sergei raised an eyebrow at him in question. "Natasha hasn't been nice to anyone but you for a while. You pay for her schooling and you gave her a credit card for her expenses." Nikolai put the word expenses in air quotes. "Do you have any idea how much of your money she spends every month?"

"No. She shouldn't have to spend much. I own the apartment she lives in and I pay the utilities and her schooling costs. Groceries should be the only thing she has to pay."

Nikolai scoffed, then started laughing almost hysterically. Another person dressed in a SWAT costume joined their group, just as Nikolai started winding down.

"What'd I miss?"

"Brandon. Glad you made it." Sergei said after giving Nikolai one more bewildered look. "Everyone, this is my assistant Brandon. I asked him to join us this evening." Sergei took a moment to make the introductions around the table. "Have a seat, Brandon." Turning back to Nikolai, "Now, why is it so funny about me thinking Natasha only spends money on groceries with the credit card I gave her?"

Brandon scoffed, much as Nikolai had, as he took the only empty chair remaining between Will and Nikolai. The noise Brandon made sent Nikolai into another fit of laughter. He focused his attention back on Brandon. "Somebody want to tell me what's so funny? Brandon?"

"Sir?"

"How much does Natasha spend a month on the credit card I gave her for necessities?"

"Um, the bill for September was for six thousand dollars."

"Holy shit," Saul said as Lee choked on his drink. Saul reached out and patted Lee on the back. "Six thousand dollars in one month?"

"Yeah. This was actually a good month. It's usually closer to ten."

"What?" Sergei was incredulous. "How does she spend that much money in a month, and why didn't you tell me?"

Brandon gave him a wide-eyed look in return. "Because I like my head attached to my body? Nobody can say anything negative about Natasha or you go into Papa Bear mode."

Sergei rubbed his temples with both hands. "What does she spend so much money on?"

Brandon shrugged. "Clothes usually. Food and drink for her and her friends at restaurants and bars. Last month, it looks like she repaired her boyfriend's car."

"I will need to talk to her. That's not what the card is supposed to be for. It's only supposed to be used for groceries and household items. Any entertainment expenses she's supposed to pay."

"Have you told *her* that?" Nikolai asked with a snicker. "And can I be there when you tell her? She's going to lose her mind."

"I told her that when I gave her the card. She must've simply forgotten."

Brandon and Nikolai both snorted before looking at each other in surprise then bursting into laughter. Sergei noted the blush spreading across Brandon's face as they made eye contact, after they had finished laughing. *Maybe there is something to Stuart's theory that there is an attraction between them.*

Sergei gave them both a stern look. "I expect one of you to tell me in future if Natasha does something you feel is extreme. As you know, I don't even look at the bills as they come in. I rely on the two of you to tell me these things."

"I want a safe word then," Nikolai countered.

"What?" Sergei was so very confused, as everyone around the table started chuckling.

"Like in BDSM. You know, for when you go all Dommy on our asses. We want a safe word, so you don't bite our heads off or make our lives miserable. Don't kill the messenger, dude."

Sergei dropped his head into his hand before looking back up at Nikolai. "Have you been reading gay romance books again?"

Nikolai gave him a wounded look and placed his hand on his heart. "I always read gay romance books. I need to feed my soul somehow."

Suddenly everyone was roaring with laughter. Kirk was laughing so hard that he had tears rolling down his face.

"Sergei," Kirk gasped out, "you should see your face. It's like you just walked in on your parents having sex."

Nikolai looked smug when Sergei looked back at him. He straightened up and sniffed loudly. "You know, you all used to fear me."

"Yeah. Well, that's what happens when you get friends, asshole," Saul responded.

Stuart leaned in and gave him a peck on the cheek. "Welcome to the family." Sergei whipped his head around to look at Stuart. "I'm kind of a package deal, just like Nikolai and Natasha are part of yours."

Sergei leaned his forehead against Stuart's with a sigh. "I'm not sure who's getting the worse end of that deal, but as long as I get you, it's worth it."

A chorus of *aw-ws* went around the table, making Sergei sit up straight again and wave his pointer finger between Nikolai and Brandon. "As for you two, I can't believe I'm saying this, but your safe word will be 'Moscow'. If you have something to tell me that you don't think I want to hear, start the conversation with 'Moscow' so I know it's serious and I need to listen objectively."

"That's so awesome. I'm so excited." Nikolai was bouncing in his seat in his enthusiasm.

"Do *not* overuse it. It's for serious situations."

"Yes, sir," Brandon agreed respectfully.

"Sure thing, boss man," Nikolai responded while batting his eyelashes at him.

Sergei shook his head at Nikolai's antics.

"What do you do for Sergei, Nikolai?" Kirk asked.

Nikolai sat up and looked serious as he answered Kirk's question. "Sergei let me intern at his company this past year. Currently I'm getting my doctorate in finance. I'm working on my dissertation. I've completed all my classwork."

"Really? Are you going to work for Sergei full-time afterward?"

"No. I don't want to go the corporate route. I really want to help people. I volunteer down at the community center with their debt management programs. I want to combine it with a small business where I can really make a difference. Right now, I'm busy trying to find a new apartment and a part-time job for expenses as I finish up my dissertation."

"Huh? Why do you need an apartment?" Sergei asked. "I thought you loved your place?"

"My landlord has decided to let his son have it, so I have to move. It's not a big deal."

"You should have said something. I have — "

"One, you don't have any apartments available anywhere near campus, and two, you've already done more than enough for me, Sergei. I'll figure it out."

"I might have a solution to both your problems," Kirk interjected.

"Really? How?"

"Everyone's Mechanic needs a front desk person and bookkeeper. The garage has gotten very busy and I hate paperwork. If you would be interested in taking over the books and man the front desk when you have time, I can let you live in the apartment over the garage. It's sitting empty now that Lee is living with Saul."

"Lee did a great job on renovating the apartment. I think you would really like it," Stuart added.

"How much would the rent be?" Nikolai bit into his bottom lip after he asked the question. It was a nervous habit that was a prime indicator of exactly how stressed he was about something. The amount of gnawing let Sergei know that Nikolai was very worried about his current situation.

"We can discuss it later. Why don't you come by the garage about ten tomorrow morning? The garage is closed, but it would give us time to go over everything."

"Ten works for me. I'll meet you there. Thank you."

"When do you have to be out of your current place?"

"November fifteenth."

"Well, the timing should work then, if you like it."

Sergei watched as the stress lines around Nikolai's eyes relaxed. He hadn't realized they were even there until they were gone. Now that he was looking, he realized Nikolai had lost some weight as well — weight he certainly didn't need to lose. He obviously needed to keep better track of his cousin.

The conversation was interrupted by the waitress bringing their drinks then getting everyone's food orders. Conversations after that were a lot less serious and they finished eating just in time to hear the band start to play from outside on the heated patio.

"Come on, everyone. It's time to dance," Nikolai jumped up and made a beeline for the dance floor. The others got up and followed him a little more slowly. Sergei made note of the bar just outside the door, where there were people lined up waiting for drinks as well as another one located just inside. Both were hopping. The bartenders were struggling to keep up, but they were doing it with smiles on their faces. The wait staff were all in the logoed T-shirts and black shorts uniforms of the place. Most had accessorized with animal ears or hats for the occasion, though.

Sergei's attention was caught by the swaying of his boyfriend's hips to the beat of the music. It had seriously been too long since he'd had his boyfriend naked. He was going to have to see if he could find a way to be home more often — or for Stuart to maybe go with him on some of these trips. He missed him badly when they weren't together. It was a weird feeling, to be sure — and one he had never felt before with anyone he'd dated.

Once they reached the dance floor, Sergei reached out, grabbed Stuart's hips and pulled him in snug against his. Wrapping his arms around Stuart, Sergei swayed their bodies together in time to the beat. Stuart turned and draped his arms over Sergei's shoulders before leaning in to whisper-shout in his ear.

"Hey, good looking, come here often?"

Sergei chuckled at Stuart's bad line before leaning in to answer. "That was bad, very, very bad." Sergei took the opportunity to run his nose up Stuart's neck before nibbling on his earlobe. His neck and ears were definite hotspots for his boyfriend, and he grinned to himself when he felt Stuart shudder and a definite bulge start to appear under his costume. Luckily Stuart's costume was baggy, so it wouldn't show, but Sergei could feel what their proximity was doing to Stuart. He was thankful he wasn't the only one feeling the heat—and he wasn't talking about the temperature on the dance floor, either. He leaned in again and spoke in Stuart's ear. "I missed you, *kotik*."

Sergei received a blinding smile in response, making his heart skip a beat. "Two more songs, then I think we'll have been social enough. I missed you too." Stuart initiated the kiss between them this time, and Sergei found himself tightening his arms around Stuart's waist and moaning into his mouth.

"Are you sure we have to wait two more songs?" Sergei asked breathlessly after Stuart pulled away.

Stuart grinned at him then spun away to dance with Lee and Nikolai, doing some complicated dance maneuvers while waving his hands in the air. Even in the ridiculous Tigger costume, Stuart was breathtaking. The joy on his face was amazing to see. Someone bumped him and it wasn't until that moment that he realized he had stopped dancing to watch his boyfriend.

Sergei looked around for Saul, Will, Kirk, Eric and Brandon, since he didn't see them on the dance floor. Finally locating them in a booth against the wall, he made his way over to where they were. Eric scooted in closer to Kirk on the seat, making room for Sergei to sit down. Sergei's eyes were drawn back to where the other three were dancing. He noticed he wasn't the only one watching the show. As he watched, a man danced up behind Stuart and slid his hands onto Stuart's hips. Sergei went to stand up, but Eric grabbed his arm and pulled him back into the booth. Sergei threw a glare over his shoulder at Eric, only to find him laughing at him.

"Stuart can handle himself. He's not interested in anyone but you. Relax."

Sergei settled himself with a sigh. Glancing back, he saw Stuart had moved in between Nikolai and Lee and was currently busy unzipping his Tigger costume and tying the arms around his waist to hold the costume up. His naked chest was now on display.

Eric chuckled near his ear. "You might want to close your mouth. You're drooling."

"You have it bad, my friend," Kirk shouted over the music.

Sergei nodded. "I do."

Saul joined the conversation. "They're beautiful together. The redhead, the blond and the brunette. All different body types and personalities."

Sergei shot a look at Brandon to find his gaze glued to Nikolai. *Yeah, there's definitely something there.* He sat back and relaxed, listening to the music and watching his boyfriend dance.

Chapter Nine

Stuart chuckled to himself as he watched Sergei out of the corner of his eye when he stripped off the top half of his costume. He looked absolutely stunned and Stuart found his self-confidence skyrocketing as he saw the effect he had on his boyfriend. *Boyfriend.* Such a simple word, and yet so life-altering. The three of them danced to song after song. It felt good to let loose like this. Stuart could feel Sergei's heated gaze on him. He had danced way more than the two songs he and Sergei had agreed to, so Sergei must be enjoying the show. Stuart was thrown out of his relaxed state when he was bumped roughly from behind and would have fallen if it weren't for Lee standing in front of him. Lee quickly steadied him, and Stuart spun around to find Natasha smirking at him as the music ended and the band announced a short break.

"Oops. Sorry. Accident." The look on Natasha's face didn't say accident or sorry, though. It said malicious glee.

"No big deal," Stuart said carefully. "It's crowded out here."

"Yep." With a head toss, Natasha was gone as quickly as she had appeared.

"That girl has issues. I mean, I don't get it. Her brother has spoiled her rotten and she still acts like a jealous twit if someone has something she doesn't."

"Yeah. That was not a friendly face," Lee added. "I'd watch out for that one."

"That was Sergei's sister Natasha. I noticed that she made sure her back was to Sergei so he couldn't see her face," Nikolai said with a wave in the direction of the booth. "Lee's right. Watch your back with her. I hate to say it, since she's my cousin and all, but she has a definite mean streak."

The three turned and made their way over to the booth with the others.

"Are you okay, Stuart?" Kirk asked. "I saw Natasha knock into you. I was surprised to see you fall forward like that."

"Yeah, she hit me pretty hard. It was no big deal. Lee caught me." Stuart looked in Lee's direction and batted his eyelashes at him. "My hero."

"What did she say to you?" Sergei asked once the chuckles had died down.

"She was sorry she bumped me. That's all." Stuart leaned in and gave Sergei a peck on the lips. "Now. I danced way more than two songs. Are you ready to go?" Stuart heard his phone ring from Sergei's suit coat breast pocket with his best friend Paul's ringtone, a Disney theme song. Stuart reached over and grabbed it, making sure to cop a feel of Sergei's hard pec as he did so. He chuckled as he hit the button to answer and held the phone to his ear.

"What's up, Paulie?"

"Hey, Stu-Stu. How goes it?"

"It goes good. I'm at a Halloween party at Puzzles with the gang. You're lucky that I heard the phone. The band is taking a break or I wouldn't have."

"Oh crap. I forgot that you might be out celebrating."

"It's all good. Was there something you needed or can I call you tomorrow?"

"Well…"

"Uh-oh. It's never good when you start a conversation like that. Spill it."

"You know how we decided we were going to spend Christmas in Florida this year rather than go to Chicago to stay with Chloe's family?"

"Yeah. Now that you have two kids under the age of four, it'd be just be too hard to do it."

"Exactly. Chloe wants our family to have our own Christmas traditions and for them to be able to open all their gifts etcetera in the comfort of their own home, instead of us having to shuffle from house to house, because God forbid anyone should come to where we are after we just took flights and who knows what else to get there. Anyway, I digress. The bottom line is negotiations have ended with us having to go up for Thanksgiving so we can stay home for Christmas. At least Thanksgiving's all at one house."

"Oh."

"Yeah, oh. I know we always spend Thanksgiving together, buddy, but this year we want you to come down for New Year's instead. Would that work?"

Stuart swallowed hard. "Yeah, that would work. I can find something else to do for Thanksgiving. Don't worry." Stuart made himself laugh, but it was obviously forced.

"I know," Paul sighed. "It's not ideal. I love Thanksgiving with you, but this means we at least have the time between Christmas and New Year's. Right? That's usually your slow time of year anyway. Why don't you come down the day after Christmas and stay until New Year's and enjoy the nice weather?"

Stuart perked up at the thought. "Yeah?"

"Yeah. Bring the new boyfriend so I can meet him and give him the 'hurt you and face the wrath of Chloe' speech."

Stuart had to laugh. Chloe was a kickass lawyer and a person to be respected and feared indeed. "Okay. I'll ask him."

"Phew. Thanks for agreeing. I know you're at a party and that Sergei just got back. I'll let you go. We can talk at our normal time tomorrow."

"Will do. Talk to you tomorrow."

Stuart hung up the phone to find everyone watching him. "What?"

"What's going on?" Lee asked. "You looked like someone kicked you in the 'nads for a moment there."

"Um, it's all good. I usually go to my friend Paul's house for Thanksgiving, but this year they're flying to Chicago to visit family so they don't have to travel for Christmas." Stuart shrugged and tried to be nonchalant about it.

Lee's face lit up. "Great! Then you can come to our Thanksgiving. Saul's family is all going down to Florida for that week this year. It's his sister Lucia's turn to host, but it's my turn to cover the Friday after the holiday at the garage, so we can't go."

It turned out Sergei's family was also going out of town to Sean's sister's house, so Sergei was going to be at loose ends too.

"Why didn't you say anything?" Stuart asked him.

"It's a month away. I figured there was time to discuss it," Sergei replied.

"Kirk and I don't have any plans this year either. My aunt broke her hip and my mom is down in New Orleans helping her. She actually plans to stay there until after she finishes physical therapy. Right now, that's not scheduled to be until after the New Year."

"Great." Lee clapped his hands together. "More people. Anyone else need somewhere to go for Thanksgiving? Brandon? Nikolai? Will?"

Brandon looked overwhelmed for a moment. "Are you serious?"

"Why wouldn't I be serious? Do you want to come? Do you have somewhere else to be?"

"No." Brandon hung his head. "I was in foster care. I don't have any family, so I've got nowhere to go. I usually eat something at home."

"Well, now you don't have to. Get the address from Sergei. Come casual. It'll be very chill. Football on the television and lots of food. Saul loves to cook."

"Wait," Sergei interrupted. "You invited all these people over for Thanksgiving and you aren't doing the cooking?"

Saul held up his hand to stop Sergei. "Believe me… You don't want Lee to do the cooking. He can do breakfast. That's about it."

Stuart took the opportunity as everyone was laughing to look around at his friends. He was so thankful to have them in his life. "Okay. So, what can we bring?"

That started a whole discussion, interrupted by the return of the band. Sergei shouted to be heard by the group. "I think that's our cue to leave. I'm in desperate need of some alone time with my boyfriend."

Stuart climbed out of the booth and extended a hand down to Sergei to help him up. Sergei stood then reached down to untie the arms holding up his costume. "You might want to put this back on. It's a bit chilly to be running around without a top on."

Stuart chuckled as Sergei used the act of helping him back into his costume to sneak a peek down at his jockstrap. Sergei groaned before pulling the zipper up on the costume and pulling him in tight so he could talk in Stuart's ear. "Holy crap. You got a tiger-print jock?"

"When I do something, I go all out," Stuart replied as he pulled away, laced their fingers together and led them to the door. He made sure to put a little extra wiggle in his hips, since he knew Sergei was looking at his ass. He pushed out of the door before he turned to speak to Sergei again. "Hmm-m… Perhaps you see something you like?"

"Nope. I see something I love."

Stuart didn't get a chance to reply before Sergei spun him around as they reached the car and pressed him up against the side of it, taking his mouth in a voracious kiss. Sergei thrust his tongue into Stuart's mouth and mapped the inside. Twining their tongues together in a duel for control, Stuart was more than happy to give up and let Sergei win this time. He had missed Sergei and couldn't wait to be naked and taken.

A few moments later, Sergei pulled away with a gasp. "Get in the car, *kotik*. We need to go now or I'll be taking you in the back seat."

"We are way too big to be fitting in your car's back seat, Barinov." Stuart said as he opened the passenger door and glanced into the back. "Hurry up. Let's go home and get naked."

Stuart watched with amusement as Sergei had to stop at the front of the car for a moment to adjust himself before he continued walking. He waited until he had put on his seatbelt before poking the horny bear. "Problems there, babe?"

"You drive me crazy. You know that. Be prepared to be naked as soon as we get through the door. I've waited long enough."

Stuart couldn't help but be amused by Sergei's growl. Stuart waited until Sergei started the car and pulled out of the parking lot and onto the street, before he reached up and slowly lowered the zipper on his costume, making sure Sergei heard it.

Sergei whipped his head around to look at Stuart before he clenched his hands on the steering wheel and resolutely faced forward to stare out of the windshield. Stuart noticed his boyfriend's jaw clench and decided to up the ante a little bit. He moaned as he pinched his right nipple while rubbing the left one before drifting his hand down and inside his costume. Cupping himself through his jock, he bucked his hips up into his grip.

"Stuart…" Sergei growled out.

"Yeah, babe?"

"You need to stop teasing me. I want to get us safely home, but you're not making it easy. You're hell on my concentration." Sergei reached out with his right hand and grabbed Stuart's wrist to yank his hand out of his costume and set it on the middle console. "Now behave. We're almost there."

Stuart gave an evil chuckle but stopped the torture for now and entertained himself by watching his boyfriend. He really was sex on a stick, everything he hadn't dared to hope of, for fear it would be another pipe dream.

"What are you doing now?" Sergei asked with exasperation.

"Looking at what's mine," Stuart almost whispered back.

Sergei jerked the wheel before correcting his course then throwing on the blinker to turn in to Stuart's driveway.

"Get in the house, *kotik*. Now!"

Stuart rushed to get out of the car and to the door of his house, reaching for his keys before he realized he didn't have any. He stood, enjoying the feel of the cold air on his already stiff nipples as he waited for Sergei to get out of the car and grab his bag from the back seat. Stuart held his breathe as Sergei stalked his way to the door before pushing him up against it and taking his mouth in a brief kiss. He pulled the key Stuart had given him out of his pocket and quickly unlocked the door. Sergei grabbed Stuart's arm and yanked him into the house after him before closing the door with a thud and slamming Stuart up against the back of it. If Stuart had thought the other kisses were hungry, he was mistaken. This one was ravenous.

Sergei grabbed the front of Stuart's costume in both hands. "Get this off. *Now*. Unless you want it in pieces."

Stuart quickly kicked off his shoes and stripped off the costume, making sure to take his socks with it. That left him in only his tiger-print jockstrap. He was so hard that the front of it was already soaked with his precum, and even with the jock, he had a considerable bulge. He looked up when he was done to find Sergei had been busy too, now standing in front of him clad only in his boxer briefs. Stuart's breath caught as he ogled the chiseled body of his boyfriend. His mouth filled with saliva and he had to raise a hand to it to make sure he wasn't drooling.

Sergei made eye contact with Stuart and the raw hunger in his boyfriend's gaze had Stuart squaring his shoulders and taking a step forward to try to get closer to the walking god. *How did I get so lucky? And he wants me.* Sergei's nostrils flared before he reached out a hand and extended his arm to shove Stuart back against the door, then took both hands, hooked his fingers in the sides of his boxer briefs and yanked them off. Stepping forward, he pressed their bodies together. Latching a finger in the elastic of Stuart's jockstrap, Sergei pulled it out then let it go with a snap, making him gasp at the sting then moan as he was swamped with need.

"Like that, do you?" Sergei's breath in his ear made Stuart shudder as more waves of arousal swept through him. "Turn around."

Stuart reached for the straps of his jock to strip it off as he turned, but Sergei grabbed his hands and pushed them over his head, spreading his fingers out and pressing them against the door.

"No. *I'll* do it. You keep your hands there."

Stuart moaned as Sergei's words filtered into his brain. Take-charge Sergei was a definite turn on. Sergei moved away a moment and Stuart heard the sound of a condom wrapper being opened, then Sergei pressed against his back again as he ran a finger along the elastic band he had previously snapped, following it around Stuart's hip to where it connected with the front fabric. Sergei continued to tease Stuart with light touches down and around the edge of the tiger-print pouch. Stuart was panting already, and Sergei hadn't even touched his cock yet. Stuart thrust his hips forward, trying to get Sergei's hand where he wanted it, where he needed it. "Please, Sergei... I need you."

Sergei chuckled in his ear as he leaned forward and pressed his naked body even harder to Stuart's back. "Do you think it was fair of you to tease me all night, watching you dance and knowing that all you had under your costume was a jockstrap?"

Stuart pushed back into Sergei, his boyfriend's cock wedging into the crease of his ass. Sergei gave a slow grind of his hips, flaming Stuart's arousal to epic levels. "Well, I had hoped you would make it here when you originally said you would, so we'd have time do something before we had to go to the party. I would've changed into my real costume then," Stuart got out on a long moan as he continued to move between Sergei's hard length in the crease of his ass and the hardness of the door in front of him.

"*What?*" Sergei's scandalized question made Stuart chuckle as he reached down and grabbed Sergei's hand and moved it to his already-lubed hole.

"I prepped myself for you, but see what happens when you're late?" Stuart shot a look over his shoulder so he could try to see Sergei's face as his boyfriend slid first one then a second finger into then out of his needy hole. Stuart had to whisper the next part, since while it was true, it was also a bit embarrassing to admit out loud. "I wore a butt plug all day, so I was ready. I thought of you as I prepped myself."

Sergei grabbed hold of Stuart's shoulder and spun him around so he could take his lover's mouth in a voracious kiss. Stuart shoved him back after a few minutes and turned back around, sticking his ass back in invitation.

"Come on, Sergei. I need. It's been too long."

Sergei dropped his forehead to Stuart's shoulder as he lined his cock up with said hungry hole and entered Stuart with one hard push. Stuart braced his hands on the door and pushed back until Sergei was as deep as he could go, his boyfriend's pubic hairs rubbing his ass and Sergei's balls pressing against his taint.

Stuart moaned as Sergei swiveled his hips, grinding hard and hitting all the best spots inside him. Stuart clenched his ass, making Sergei gasp behind him and freeze.

"You need to stop that or I'm not going to make it much longer. You've teased me all night. I'm on the edge here."

"Aw, poor Sergei," Stuart retorted while clenching and releasing his ass in pulses, milking his cock.

"That's not nice, *kotik*."

"You forget that kittens have claws, Sergei."

"I'll try to remember in future. Now relax so I can move and give us what we both need."

Stuart relaxed and tilted his hips a bit more to get the perfect angle so Sergei would hit his prostate with every thrust. Sergei stood up straight and gripped Stuart's hips hard enough that he would have bruises, but that was okay. He'd missed Sergei. He needed him to re-stake his claim, to remind him how good they were together. "I missed you. *Please*."

Sergei reached around and pulled Stuart's jock out and over his hard cock, nestling it under his balls. Then Sergei grabbed Stuart's aching shaft, his hand moving smoothly with all the precum dripping from the head and coating it.

"Oh. My. God. Just like that. Please, Sergei, I need to come. Shit. Right. Fucking. There."

"Now, Stuart. Come right the fuck *now!*" Sergei's words then switched to Russian, but Stuart probably wouldn't have understood even if he was still speaking in English, as just at that moment his balls pulled up and emptied with hard pulses onto the back of the door.

Sergei released his cock and put his hand back on Stuart's hip as he shoved into Stuart's hole once, twice, three more times before grinding their hips together and releasing into the condom with a shout. Stuart dropped his head to the door as Sergei collapsed against his back, dropping his forehead again to rest on Stuart's shoulder.

"Hey, Sergei," Stuart whispered.

"Yeah?" Sergei whispered back.

"Welcome back."

Sergei chuckled against Stuart's neck as he raised his head up enough to place a kiss where his boyfriend's neck met his shoulder. "It's good to be home, *kotik*. It's good to be home. Now come on. Let's clean up. I need to hold you while we sleep. I sleep better with you in my arms."

Stuart groaned as Sergei slowly pulled his softening cock out and stepped back. He stripped his jock the rest of the way off. Now that he wasn't horny as hell, it wasn't very comfortable rubbing under his balls. He went to the kitchen to wet a dishtowel and wipe himself down as Sergei made his way to the half-bath to dispose of the condom. Once he was done with a cursory wipe down, since he was hoping to talk Sergei into jumping into the shower with him, he wet the towel again to clean up the mess on the back of the door. Sergei had been busy collecting the discarded clothing and draping it all over his arm.

Stuart made his way over to the door with the damp cloth and the cleaner he had grabbed from under the kitchen sink. His head came up when he heard Sergei chuckling behind him. "What?"

"You. Making sure to do a thorough job of everything you do."

Stuart's cheeks heated as he turned his attention back to the door. "My uncle always used to tell me that if you don't have time to do it right the first time, you certainly don't have time to redo it."

"Your uncle? The one you stayed with on breaks? You don't talk about him much."

Stuart shrugged, as he took one more swipe at the door to make sure he'd gotten everything before returning the cleaner to the kitchen, throwing the dirty towel into the laundry room around the corner then rejoining Sergei in the foyer to continue the conversation. "I only knew him from the time I was eighteen until I was twenty-nine and we were both really busy, so we didn't get a chance to spend a lot of time together. He was a social worker who worked a ton of hours. I worked three jobs over the summers to make enough money for school while I was in college."

Stuart laced their fingers together and pulled Sergei behind him up the stairs to the master bath, continuing the story as he went. "After college, I worked two jobs, because I always knew I wanted to open my own business. One job was with a large web design company to get the experience I needed. The other was at an electronics retailer, working for their tech support group. That gave me an employee discount that I could use to purchase the hardware and software I would need. I was getting ready to put in my notice and start my own business when Peter got his lung cancer diagnosis. The doctors didn't find the cancer until it was stage four. I tried to spend as much time as possible with him then, but he was only alive three months after that. The chemo made him so sick. It was really rough." Stuart took a moment to swallow hard, before releasing Sergei's hand so he could start the shower.

"It sounds like you miss him."

Stuart glanced over his shoulder to find Sergei sorting their clothes into his different laundry baskets. One was for dry cleaning, one for colors, one for whites. *My tendency to organize things to death shows in here,* he thought as he shook his head at himself.

"I do. I mean, he took me in. He listened and gave me advice without being pushy about it. The only thing he asked me for was money toward groceries. After he died, I found out that he had been putting all the money I gave him into a savings account for me. He left me everything except his house. He donated that to this guy he knew who wanted to set up a halfway house to help people get back on their feet after prison. I wanted to be closer to downtown, so it worked out well anyway."

Stuart stepped into the warm water of the shower and stuck his head under the stream to wet his hair. He had gotten quite sweaty from dancing and their other activities. When he went to reach for his shampoo, it wasn't where it was supposed to be.

"Looking for this?" Sergei said from behind him.

Stuart opened his eyes to find Sergei shaking the shampoo bottle at him, before pouring some into his hand and replacing the bottle where it went. Sergei put both hands into Stuart's hair and worked up a lather.

"Was your uncle a neat freak too?"

Stuart gave an exasperated huff, while trying not to melt into a pile of goo with Sergei's gentle hair wash. "If by a neat freak you mean that I could find whatever I was looking for at his house then yes. He liked to have a place for everything and everything in its place."

Sergei chuckled. "Were your mom and stepfather not that way?"

Stuart choked on his laughter. "My mother loves her knick-knacks. She has all sorts of collections and other things that cover every available space, mostly religious items. She has this entire cabinet full of ceramic nuns alone." Stuart shuddered thinking about it. "She's not even Catholic. Anyway, my stepfather is always afraid he might need something at some future time and refuses to throw anything away."

"That must've been hard for you."

"Yeah. I kept my room neat. It drove my mother crazy."

Sergei smirked at him as he tipped Stuart's head back to rinse out the suds. "That's not a problem most mothers have, their child being too neat."

"I know, right?"

Sergei picked up the bar of soap and the washcloth and used both to clean Stuart from top to bottom. Stuart's member gave a semi-interested twitch when Sergei got to his cock and balls, but its glimmer of interest was quickly followed by Stuart's yawn. "Sorry. I'm not twenty anymore. I guess dinner, dancing and sex are the limit for me." Another yawn followed that statement.

Sergei shoved him back under the water to rinse, before turning him toward the opening to the shower.

"Go on and dry off then get ready for bed. I'll meet you in there after I wash."

"You don't want me to return the favor?"

"This was for you, *kotik*. You look dead on your feet."

"Yeah. I got used to you sleeping with me. It was weird when you weren't there." They hadn't spent very many nights apart since they'd started sleeping together. Stuart usually ended up at Sergei's or Sergei at his house. He hadn't really realized it until Sergei hadn't been there this past week. Stuart leaned forward and gave Sergei a peck on the lips. The kiss was one of affection. "See you in there."

Stuart took a few moments after toweling off to do all his nightly rituals before he shot one more glance in his boyfriend's direction and made his way to the bed. He was asleep as soon as his head hit the pillow.

Chapter Ten

Sergei stopped in the doorway to look at his sleeping boyfriend. As usual, he had one foot stuck out from under the covers. It was one of Stuart's quirks that he had grown to love. He said it helped regulate his body temperature as he slept. As long as it meant Sergei could hold him in his arms at night, he didn't care. Sergei had missed Stuart while he'd been gone. It was not a feeling Sergei was familiar with having. He had never dated anyone for long. He had a reputation, in fact, of being coolly detached. If any of the previous people he'd dated, male or female, made demands, he left. He didn't care. With Stuart, he was in uncharted waters and struggling to find his footing.

Switching off the light, he made his way to the left side of the bed and climbed in next to Stuart. Sound asleep, Stuart still rolled over immediately and snuggled into him, resting his head on Sergei's chest. Sergei put his arms around him and started to run his hand through his hair. He loved their quiet moments like this. Stuart was a definite snuggler in bed, very much resembling his kitten nickname.

Thinking back on the evening, he had to smile. The smile dropped from his face as he thought about Natasha and her behavior, though. He had watched as her boyfriend had become more and more drunk as the evening had worn on. Natasha hadn't been exactly sober either. She had just turned twenty-one a couple of weeks before, but she wasn't an amateur. She had given him a haughty glare when she'd caught him watching her do a no-hands shot. He didn't know what he was going to do about her. She seemed a little out of control.

Stuart must have felt him tense, because he petted his chest and whispered a quiet, "Shush, babe. Go to sleep."

Sergei tightened his grip around Stuart for a moment before leaning his head down and taking a deep inhale of Stuart's scent. The combination of the tea tree shampoo he used, along with Stuart's own unique musk, calmed him and he willed himself to relax and enjoy the moment with his boyfriend. Taking another deep breath, Sergei allowed himself to fall asleep.

* * * *

Sergei slept hard until his alarm went off at seven the next morning. Rolling over, he realized he was alone in the bed. He listened for a moment to try to determine where Stuart could be. Not hearing anything, he grumbled as he stretched, made a trip to the restroom then pulled on his boxers before he went in search of his boyfriend. Following the smell of coffee and other delicious things to the kitchen, he found Stuart at the stove plating pancakes, eggs and bacon.

Stuart glanced over his shoulder at Sergei as he walked in the door. "I was going to come wake you for breakfast in a couple of minutes. I woke up starving. I figured you would be too."

Sergei walked up behind Stuart and embraced him from behind. "I definitely could eat, but I didn't like waking to a lonely bed."

Stuart turned his head to kiss Sergei's cheek. "Aww, poor Pooh Bear."

Sergei pulled his head back in shock. "Pooh Bear? Really?"

"Well, if I'm Tigger, I figured that makes you Pooh," Stuart said with a smirk before returning his attention to his cooking.

"I always thought Tigger and Rabbit had a thing going."

Sergei enjoyed the slow pan and look of disbelief he received from his boyfriend.

"What?"

"Well, Tigger was always picking on Rabbit. I figured it was like pulling pigtails." Sergei hid his smile by releasing Stuart and making his way over to pour himself a cup of coffee. He smiled wider when he heard Stuart spluttering behind him.

"Oh. My. God. You've actually given this some thought."

Turning, Sergei leaned against the counter, raising an eyebrow in question. "Haven't you?"

"Well, no, but now I can't think of anything else. Who was with Pooh then?"

"Not sure. Eeyore, maybe. Eeyore's doom and gloom versus Pooh's positive outlook? I heard Pooh is actually a girl bear, so maybe that would work."

Stuart roared with laughter as he turned off the stove and walked toward the breakfast nook with two full plates. Sergei belatedly noticed the table had already been set with silverware and glasses of juice. "Wow. You've been busy. This looks great."

"Thanks. It was nice having someone to cook for. Have a seat. Let's eat while it's hot."

The men were silent as they ate. Sergei realized he was indeed starving once he took the first bite. Finally sated, he leaned back in his chair with his cup of coffee in hand and watched his boyfriend mop up the last bit of syrup on his plate with his last bite of pancake.

Stuart looked up at him and raised his eyebrows in obvious question.

"I like looking at you," Sergei said with a shrug.

Stuart waved him off as he sat back with his glass of juice. "Back to our earlier discussion. Here's the question then. If I'm Tigger, that makes you Rabbit. Is that what we've decided?"

Sergei grinned. "Yep. If you'd like, a common Russian endearment is *zaichonok*. It means bunny, but it also kind of indicates, um…"

"Great sexual prowess?"

"Yeah…that." Sergei's cheeks warmed. *Am I blushing?*

"Are you blushing?" Stuart asked incredulously. After a moment he obviously decided to take pity on him. "Okay, so we got babe and *zaichonok* for you now. Awesome."

Sergei laughed. "Your accent is terrible."

"Eh. I'll have time to practice. It's all good. What's on the agenda today?"

"There isn't anything on the agenda. There is no Sunday dinner since my mother is away at a conference."

"You mean we can hang out naked all day? Just the two of us?" Stuart waggled his eyebrows at Sergei, making him laugh.

"I like the way you think." Sergei stood and placed a quick kiss on Stuart's cheek before grabbing the items that needed to be returned to the refrigerator, while Stuart took care of the plates. It didn't take long with them working together to get the kitchen put to rights.

Stuart disappeared for a moment before meeting Sergei in the living room with a bedsheet, which he laid on the couch. He then stripped off his boxers, climbed on the couch first and sat with his back in one of the corners. Patting his chest, he encouraged Sergei to sit in front of him. Sergei did as he was told after stripping off his own boxers, and he sat with his back to Stuart's front. He leaned back in Stuart's embrace with a sigh.

"What was the sigh for, babe?" Stuart reached out, grabbed the blanket off the back of the couch and spread it over the two of them as he asked the question.

Sergei snuggled in deeper. "It makes me happy that you're not that much smaller than me, so this is possible without me crushing you."

"Dated a lot of twinks, have you?"

"You know I have — and a lot of needy women too. You're very comfy."

Stuart's soft chuckle in his ear made him shiver. "Glad to be of service."

Sergei distantly heard the sound of his phone ringing from where he'd left it in Stuart's bedroom.

With a groan, he reluctantly threw off the blanket, stood up and pulled his boxers back on. "That's Brandon's ringtone. He doesn't usually call me on Sundays. He knows it's my family day. I'd better see what he needs." Sergei tucked Stuart back in and made his way up the stairs to grab his phone. It had stopped ringing but started up again almost immediately. He snatched up the phone off the charger and answered. "What's going on, Brandon?"

"Um, I don't know how to tell you this, so I'm just going to say it right out. I just received a phone call from front desk security. Someone named Katia called, claiming to be your sister. Security said she had a heavy Russian accent. She says your father, Pyotr, is here in the US. He was presenting a paper at a conference when he collapsed. He is currently at Duke, getting treatment for a heart valve issue. She said she was calling for two reasons. One, your father would like to see you and your mother, and two, you need to be tested, since the doctors say it's genetic."

Sergei waited until Brandon had paused and remained silent for a count of three before trying to respond. His mind was reeling with all the information his assistant had given him. "Did she leave a number where I can reach her?" He was glad that his voice came out calm and detached.

"I'll text it to you now. I'm sorry to bother you on Sunday."

"No. You did the right thing. Now, go enjoy your day."

"Yes, sir."

Sergei sat on the bed in deep thought until he heard shuffling footsteps coming down the hallway, looking up in time to see Stuart fill the doorway. He had to smile when he saw Stuart standing there with the blanket wrapped around him.

"What? I got cold without you. What's up, babe?"

He stared back down at his hands as he relayed the conversation with Brandon.

Stuart came to join him on the bed, wrapping the blanket around the both of them before jumping away when they touched. "God, you're freezing. Get under the covers." Stuart stood up and grabbed Sergei's arm to make him stand so he could lift up the covers then push Sergei onto the bed. He followed his boyfriend and pulled the covers up and over the two of them. Once covered, Stuart yanked Sergei into his arms and started rubbing his hands up and down his back to warm him.

Sergei had been too surprised by the maneuver to react, but as he realized exactly how cold he had become, he burrowed down into Stuart's warmth, reveling in the quiet comfort.

"Do you know who this Katia is?"

"Yes, I made it my business to know everything about Pyotr. Katia is Pytor's daughter with his wife. She is the oldest."

"Ah. What're you going to do?"

"I'm not going to let my mother anywhere near him until I find out what his game is. That's for sure."

"Well, that goes without saying," Stuart huffed. "What else?"

"I guess I'll call Katia back and see what I can find out. Stay with me while I do it?"

"Whatever you need."

"You. I just need you."

Stuart placed a kiss on the top of his head before tightening his grip around him in a hug.

"Why do I even care? He wasn't ever a father to me. He used my mother. I don't think he ever really cared for her either — only what she could do for him."

"Because you're a decent human being, no matter what reports say to the contrary."

Sergei had to crack a smile at Stuart's declaration. "Yeah. I guess I do have a bit of a reputation."

"Just a bit." Stuart placed another gentle kiss on the top of his head and resumed rubbing his hands up and down Sergei's back. "It's funny, though. You have a Pyotr in your life who was the worst thing for you, and I had a Peter in mine who was the best."

"Irony for sure. I really didn't think I would ever have to deal with or see him again."

"You're not a little boy anymore. You can handle it."

"Yeah. Thank you."

"For what?"

"Being a supportive boyfriend."

"That's what boyfriends are for, right?"

Sergei heard a text come in on his phone and sighed before reaching outside their cocoon to snag the phone from where he had placed it on the bedside table. He made no attempt to leave his perch on Stuart's chest, though. If he had to deal with this, he would do it from a position of comfort.

He pulled up the text from Brandon with the forwarded phone number. He hesitated a moment before pressing the button to connect a call, then hung up after a few minutes' conversation in Russian.

"Feel like going to the hospital with me?"

"Is he really there?"

"Yeah. It seems they need to repair the valve and try to treat some of the damage done to his heart. I guess he's been having issues for a while, but he ignored it.

He waited too long to get it looked at. Visiting hours go until nine tonight. Surgery is in the morning."

"Okay. What do you want to do?"

"*Want* to do? Stay here in bed with you. *Will* do? I guess I should go to the hospital and at least to get the details of what I should be tested for."

"Okay. Then that's what we'll do. I know your mom is at a conference, but you should call her too. She'll be pissed if you don't tell her right away."

"Yeah. Well, I need to stop at my place to get a different suit to wear before we go too."

"Power suit time?" Stuart asked, bending his head so he could look Sergei in the face.

"You know it."

"Okay, but let's stay here for a few more minutes, then we'll shower and get a move on. You can reward my good supportive boyfriend awesomeness with lunch out."

"Deal, *kotik*." Sergei snuggled in and enjoyed the feeling of Stuart running his fingers through his hair. After about ten minutes, he gave another deep sigh before sitting up and leaning back against the headboard. "I can't call my mother while snuggling with you."

"Agreed," Stuart said as he sat up next to him. "I'll go jump in the shower while you talk to her. Okay?"

"Yep." Sergei pulled up his contact list and found the entry for his mother. He pressed Connect as he watched Stuart walk to the bathroom. *Damn, my boyfriend is hot.* The phone rang twice before it was picked up.

"Hello, my Sergei. How are you?"

"I'm good, Mama."

His mother switched to Russian as the noise levels around her dropped. She was obviously walking somewhere quieter as she talked. "You have your serious voice on. What's wrong?"

"I got a phone call from Pyotr's daughter." He refused to call her his sister. "Pyotr is here at Duke. He was in town presenting a paper at a conference when he collapsed. I guess he has a heart valve issue. He wants to see us, and he wanted to tell me so I could get tested too. It seems the doctors say it's genetic." There was silence on the other end of the phone. "Mama? Did you hear me?"

"I heard you. I assume you are going to see him?"

"Only to find out what I should be tested for. He was never my father."

"Sergei —" his mother began.

"No, Mama! He never cared. You know he didn't. He didn't even want his name on my birth certificate."

"And that was his loss. I come back on Wednesday. If he is still in hospital, tell him Sean and I will come see him then. He has no power over us, Sergei. Show him what true power is. Go in there in full Barinov mode."

"Yes, Mama. I am stopping at my house for my best power suit before we go to the hospital."

"Ah, are you at Stuart's then?"

"Yes, Mama. He's going to go with me to the hospital."

"Tell him he's a good boy."

That startled a laugh out of him. "I will, Mama."

"Good. Call me after you see Pyotr."

"I will. Love you, Mama."

"And I love you. I will talk to you later. Now, I have important business at the slot machines. I so love Vegas."

Sergei groaned. "Don't overdo it, Mama."

"Oh, leave me be. I'm having fun. Bye."

He hadn't noticed Stuart leaving the bathroom, but his voice came from the walk-in closet. "What do you want me to wear?"

"I don't know. Let me see what you have. I don't even know what the options are. You've never let me see your closet."

Walking in, he saw that one whole side was filled with costumes.

"Wow. You weren't kidding about having a lot of costumes."

"Nope."

"Did you already have the Tigger costume or did you have to buy it?"

Stuart pointed to the back of the closet. "I actually have the whole set already. I volunteer to do story time sometimes down at the library. The kids like it when I come in costume."

"You said you were going to change before we went last night. What were you planning to wear?"

"Oh, the pirate one," Stuart indicated a costume right next to the door. "It would have been much cooler."

"The pants would have been skintight on you."

"The shirt would have covered all the naughty bits. It would've been okay." Stuart laughed at Sergei's growl. "Never mind that now. What should I wear if you're wearing a mega power suit?"

Sergei turned his attention to the other side of the closet, which was mainly full of T-shirts, sweatshirts and jeans. Stuart's dress clothes only filled about two feet of space in the large closet. Most of that was dress shirts. Sergei moaned at the pitiful selection.

"What?"

"You only have one suit!" Sergei couldn't keep the shock out of his voice.

"I don't need more than one suit."

Sergei didn't know what Stuart saw in his expression, but it was enough to send him into hysterics.

Once he calmed down to an occasional chuckle, Sergei quirked one eyebrow at him. "Are you done?"

"Yep. All done. You should have seen your face. You looked like you were in actual pain and that you couldn't believe I only had one suit. I hate to break it to you, big guy, but most people only have one suit, two at the most."

"Well, we'll need to get you a few more if you are going to be my plus one at events — at least two more suits and a tuxedo. I have to attend a shareholder's dinner in New York City in January. The event is black tie, so you will need a tuxedo for it."

"Can't I just rent one?"

A shudder of revulsion went through his body, the obvious reaction sending Stuart into more hysterics. "No. You cannot just rent a tuxedo for the event." Waving a hand in the air. "Never mind that for now. Let's see what we have to work with for going to see Pyotr."

"I have some nice sweaters," Stuart said, pointing to a set of shelving Sergei hadn't noticed.

He found a beautiful blue crew neck cashmere sweater, which he matched with a pair of black dress slacks. Handing both items of clothing to Stuart, he watched as Stuart got dressed, pulling on first the pants over his boxer briefs then the sweater over his white undershirt. Sergei caught his breath at the look of amusement and affection in Stuart's gaze, when he glanced up as he was threading his belt through the loops.

"Do I pass inspection?"

"You're gorgeous." Sergei grabbed Stuart's hips and pulled him in closer before bending his head and giving Stuart a brief kiss, then pulled him into a hug, which Stuart returned.

"Come on, babe. Let's get to your house so you can change and we can get this over with."

"Yeah. Let's go." Sergei let go of Stuart and took a step back, waving a hand in the direction of the door. "After you."

"Why thank you, kind sir. What a gentleman."

"For now."

"What?" Stuart asked, looking back at him.

"I'm a gentleman for now. After this is over, I make no promises. I'll pack some clothes for Monday while we're at my place."

"Sounds good."

Chapter Eleven

Stuart stood in the doorway leading into the hospital room. Sergei had been even quieter than usual as they had made their way there. Gone was the laughing, joking man of earlier. In his place was the man whose reputation preceded him as someone to respect or fear — he didn't care which. He was an imposing figure, that was for sure. Stuart knew this wasn't the time, but damn, did Sergei turn him on when he got like this.

Forcing his attention away from his boyfriend before he embarrassed himself, he instead focused on the patient he assumed was Pyotr sleeping in the hospital bed. He didn't know what he had been expecting, but whatever it was, the man in the hospital bed wasn't it. Looking at him, Stuart didn't see anything of him in Sergei. Even the coloring was different. Pyotr was blond and didn't look to be taller than his own five-ten, but it was hard to gauge when he was lying in a bed.

Pyotr must have sensed them, because his eyes opened and he looked their way. "Well, I can see where you get your eye color from." Stuart smirked at the glare Sergei shot him, before reaching out and putting his hand on Sergei's back in a show of support. If he happened to use the hand to nudge Sergei a little farther into the room, well, that was a side benefit.

"Hello, Pyotr."

"Sergei."

The two men stared at each other for a long moment. Stuart was beginning to think that was all they were going to do before Pyotr finally spoke again, rattling off a sentence in Russian.

Sergei crossed his arms over his chest and stood even straighter, at his absolute most imposing.

"My boyfriend does not speak Russian. We will speak in English."

Pyotr shot a look at Stuart before continuing in heavily accented but understandable English. "It's been a long time. I have heard you are doing well for yourself."

"Yes," was Sergei's only response.. When Stuart realized that was all Sergei was going to say, he gave Sergei another nudge. Sergei harrumphed, but reluctantly added to his original answer. "I own several businesses and am well respected, but that has nothing to do with you and everything to do with how wonderful my mother is."

Pyotr opened and closed his mouth a couple of times, obviously at a loss as to how to respond. Before Pyotr could figure it out, his gaze darted to the open door as someone came up behind Stuart. Turning, he found a female version of the man in the bed. She only stood about five foot six or seven, though.

Holding out his hand, Stuart said, "You must be Katia. I'm Sergei's boyfriend Stuart."

"Yes. I'm Katia. I am Pyotr's oldest child." She shot a look at Sergei that was half challenge and half curiosity. "I did not learn of you until after my mother's death last year. When father was planning this trip, he wanted both me and my younger brother Viktor to come with him so we could meet Sergei. I did not think it would be under these circumstances, though."

"And where is Viktor?" Sergei asked.

"Unfortunately, Viktor was unable to come, as his wife is due to give birth any day now. It will be their second child. I have fraternal twins, a boy and a girl, who are now twelve. Viktor has one girl, who is six, and they are expecting a boy. Do you have children?"

"No. I have never been married and have no children as of yet."

"Oh. Because you are gay?"

"No," Sergei snapped. "Because I have only recently found someone I would consider raising a family with."

Stuart jolted in surprise and turned around to stare at Sergei. "You want to have kids?"

Sergei's gaze jerked to Stuart and softened. "Of course. I would love to have a family with you, when the time is right."

Stuart swallowed hard and nodded before offering Sergei a small smile. "I would like that — when the time is right, of course."

"Of course, but first we must find out what anomalies we could pass on to our children." Sergei turned back to Pyotr and hardened his attitude again. Katia made her way to the chair next to the bed. "What have the doctors said?"

Pyotr sighed heavily. "I have a condition called bicuspid aortic valve disease. It only affects one to two percent of the population but has been found to be genetic in families. It is twice as likely to be found in males."

"And what is that exactly?" Stuart asked.

Katia and Pyotr shared a look, then Katia continued the explanation. "From what I understand, the aortic valve should have three flaps that allow blood to flow, then the valve closes. With this defect, the valve only has two flaps. In Papa's case, the valve has not been closing properly, which has led to calcification. His heart has had to work harder, which is why when he was stressed after travel then his presentation, he passed out."

Sergei jumped in with the next question. "Okay. What is the test for it and what are the treatments? Is there medicine that can be taken?"

"No medicine… It's a heart structure issue. You need to have an echocardiogram to find out if you have it. It can only be treated surgically. There are three surgical options. One, repair the valve, which will probably have a leaking reoccurrence because the defect is not fixed. Two, replace the valve with a bioprosthetic valve. The downside of the bioprosthetic valve is that it tends to only last ten to fifteen years before it must be replaced again. The third option is to replace the valve with a mechanical valve. It should not have to ever be replaced but requires the recipient to have to take blood thinners for the rest of their life."

"Which are you doing? You're having surgery tomorrow, correct?" Sergei asked, giving Pyotr a hard stare.

"Yes, my surgery is scheduled for tomorrow morning. I am having the mechanical valve replacement. Blood thinners will be easier to get and maintain in Russia than having to schedule another heart surgery. I know I have no right to ask such a thing, but I would like it if you came to keep Katia company during the surgery. It would be a hard thing to sit and wait alone."

Stuart reached out and put his arm around Sergei's waist. "We'll be here."

"What?" Sergei's head came around and he pinned Stuart with a glare.

"Excuse us a moment." Stuart pulled Sergei into the hall to have a more private conversation. "You can call your doctor in the morning to maybe see if he can schedule your tests — whatever is needed — while we're here. That way we'll know what we're dealing with. Besides, Katia is innocent in all this. No one should have to wait alone."

Sergei stared down into Stuart's eyes for a long moment before giving a loud sigh. "Fine, but you will *not* leave me alone with her."

Stuart smirked at him. "Why? Does she scare you?"

"Not at all, but as you said, she's innocent and I can be cranky when I'm not in control of a situation."

Stuart laughed outright at the grudging admission. "Oh? Is that supposed to be a newsflash?"

Stuart reached out and yanked Sergei into a hug when he growled. He held tight until Sergei relaxed a little bit, before pulling back and giving him a gentle kiss. "Come on, babe. Let's go say goodbye then go get some lunch. We'll have to find out what time we have to be back tomorrow."

Walking back into the room, they found Pyotr and Katia with their heads close together, whispering to each other. Both turned in their direction as they crossed into the room.

"What time is the surgery tomorrow?" Sergei asked Katia.

"The surgery is scheduled for ten. I'm planning on getting here about eight, so I can see him before they take him down."

"We'll meet you here at eight tomorrow morning then." Sergei went to leave the room. Turning, he almost ran straight into Stuart.

Stuart raised his eyebrows at him and shook his head. Sergei mouthed back, "What?"

Stuart widened his eyes at Sergei, before looking around him and addressing Katia. "Is there anything we can bring you? Perhaps breakfast in the morning?"

"Oh. That would be lovely. I have a coffee maker in my room, but that is all."

"We'll grab something on our way then. Don't worry. We'll even bring the good coffee."

Katia gave Stuart a genuine smile before it dimmed when she looked at Sergei. "If it's not too much trouble."

"It will be no trouble at all."

"He'll probably ask his assistant to do it."

"That is what Brandon is for, is it not? To do what I need?" Sergei asked.

"Yes, Sergei." Rolling his eyes, Stuart grabbed Sergei's hand. "Let's go. We'll see you both tomorrow."

Making their way back to the parking garage, Stuart took a moment to observe his boyfriend. Noting the clenched jaw and tense shoulders, he made an executive decision about their next plans. "You can call your mom while I drive us back to my house. I have some leftover barbecue ribs and sides we can eat for lunch."

"What? I thought we were going out to lunch?"

"You are so wound up that I will worry for the general population if I allow you free. We are going to go to my place and have a nice lunch, then we'll work on finding a way to get you to relax."

Sergei grumbled but didn't otherwise argue, so Stuart was taking it as a win. Climbing into the car, he waited for Sergei to get settled and click his seatbelt before calling his name. "Sergei…" He waited until he looked at him. "I know that was hard. I'm proud of you." He then leaned over the console and kissed him, only leaning back when he felt Sergei relax into the kiss. "There's more of that once we get home. Call your mama. Don't worry about speaking in English. I know you have a lot to discuss with her."

"Thank you for coming with me. I do appreciate it — and you."

Stuart turned his attention to getting the car started and backing out of the parking spot. He shot Sergei a glance as he paused to put the car in Drive, "I know you do. I wouldn't want to be anywhere else."

Stuart listened to the cadence of Sergei and Daria's conversation for the entire ride home. He couldn't understand the words, but he could feel the passion and he loved the flow of the language. *Maybe one day I'll even know what they're saying.* Stuart scoffed at himself. Languages were *so* not his thing. He pulled into the garage at his house just as Sergei wrapped up his call with his mother.

"What did your mother say?"

"She said it is nice of us to keep Katia company," Sergei scoffed. "She'll be back Wednesday and will go see him then. That was basically it."

Stuart climbed out of the car and made his way to the door leading into the kitchen. "It must've been weird, seeing him as an adult after all this time."

"It was. As I said earlier, I never thought I would ever see him again, so it was a bit of a mindfuck."

"What did you think?" Stuart asked as he went to the refrigerator and started getting out the leftovers to reheat. He heard Sergei pull out one of the barstools as he put the ribs in the microwave. He turned, leaned against the counter and looked at Sergei, to find him staring at his own finger where he was tracing a line in the granite, over and over. "Well? Any thoughts about the man?"

Sergei's head snapped up. "Sorry, *kotik*. I zoned out for a moment. When I was a kid, he seemed like such a scary, fierce man. I was to be quiet when he came over and not bother him. I wasn't to speak to him unless I was spoken to—that kind of thing. Looking back on it, it was more that he didn't want to be my father. He looked at it as more of a way to control my mother. He would use something I did or said as a reason for him not to come around for a few weeks, probably when he had a family event of some kind. At the time, I thought I wasn't good enough, that I could never be good enough."

"And now?"

"Now?" Sergei paused and lowered his gaze to watch his finger drawing patterns on the granite again. "Now, he's old and small and weak. The years have certainly not been kind to him."

"And how do you feel about that?"

"Angry."

"Why angry?"

"Because I spent all this time fighting to be stronger and richer because I wanted to make sure he could never make Mama cry again — that he could never do anything to control us, that no one could" — Sergei paused to let out a self-deprecating laugh — "only to find I've prepared for a tank attack when he's riding a bicycle. All that energy was wasted."

Stuart thought about it as he pulled the food out of the microwave and split it between two plates. He set the ribs and some chips at the breakfast bar before grabbing drinks and the potato salad out of the refrigerator and going to join Sergei there. Stuart placed his hand over Sergei's and waited for his boyfriend to look at him.

"None of it was wasted. You're an amazing man. You didn't sit around feeling sorry for yourself. You set goals and you achieved them. You're too smart and driven to sit back and ever let anyone take credit for your work. You've worked hard for everything you have, and you expect the same from the people around you. You can be a bit of an asshole from time to time, but" — Stuart squeezed Sergei's hand — "you're also one of the most dedicated sons, brothers, cousins or friends I've ever seen. You care deeply. That's the difference. Yes, his rejection helped form some of who you are, but I love all the different parts of you. If it weren't for Katia, I would say that you should walk away. He can't do anything to you anymore. But give your sister a chance. She's innocent in all this. She seems like she simply wants to get to know you, and as I said, no one should have to hang out in a hospital waiting room alone."

"Wait. Did you just say you love me?"

Stuart smiled gently at Sergei. "Yeah. I did. I love you."

Sergei's eyes filled with tears, shocking Stuart. "I love you too." Leaning over, he gave Stuart a gentle kiss. It was interrupted by the sound of Sergei's stomach growling.

Stuart pulled back with a laugh. "Eat. Then we'll go upstairs and I'll give you a back rub. We'll see if we can get you to relax. Tomorrow is going to be a long day."

Sergei leaned his forehead against Stuart's for a moment. "That sounds amazing. I love you."

Stuart gave him a quick peck on the lips before sitting back. "I love you too. Now eat."

Stuart turned the conversation to less serious topics while they ate. "Somehow Sasha talked me into volunteering to help with sets for his play. I, of course, then voluntold Lee he was helping me. It's been fun, having a chance to hang with both of them. Your brother is a riot."

"Yes. I'm quite lucky to have him as a brother, but what do you mean you 'voluntold' Lee?"

"Meaning I volunteered Lee to help me then told him he was doing it."

Sergei chuckled. "Interesting. I like that. I'm going to use it."

"Yeah, well, the play is in mid-December and we are crunched for time. I've had to talk Lee out of some of his more complicated ideas. They would be amazing, but we don't have the time."

"Speaking of brothers… Did you ever find out what your brother wanted the money for?"

"Oh yeah… He thought his girlfriend was pregnant, so he wanted to buy her a ring. He used the money from the motorcycle to get the ring. He asked. She said yes, but then left him for another guy after she found out she wasn't actually pregnant. He wanted to borrow money to get a lawyer so he could get the ring back. Mom was horrified by all of it. That's the only reason I found out. Our last monthly phone call was all about the issue. I guess he finally got the ring back and was slapped with a restraining order by his ex-girlfriend, because he called her like twenty times a day, splitting the calls between begging her to come back to him and telling her to give him back the ring."

"You're kidding?"

"Nope. I wish I were. Mom was all" — Stuart switched his voice to a high-pitched one in a very bad imitation of a woman's voice — "the poor, poor dear. He works so hard. She would've been lucky to have him. He would have loved their child so-o-o much."

Sergei choked on the chip he was trying to eat. Stuart reached out and slapped him on the back to help him breathe.

"Your mother is delusional. I only met him one time, and I can tell you Andy would not handle parenthood well. Are you sure she doesn't take drugs?"

"Nope. My mom is all about the sanctity of the body God has created — no drugs, no alcohol, no cigarettes, limited caffeine. College was a total shock for me." Stuart grinned, thinking about all the things he and Paul had done and experimented with in college.

"What's that look for?" Sergei waved a rib in the direction of Stuart's face.

"Thinking about college. I didn't have a lot of free time, but Paul and I did have some fun. He'd drag me to a party occasionally."

"Paul calls you every Sunday, right?"

"Yep. About six every Sunday we FaceTime and catch up."

"It's great you two are still so close. I haven't spoken to my college roommate in years."

"That's too bad. Were you close?"

"Not really. As you said, I can be a bit of an asshole."

Stuart laughed and stood up to start cleaning the mess from lunch. "Go on upstairs, Barinov. I owe you a massage."

Chapter Twelve

Sergei woke with a start. Glancing at his watch, he realized he had been out for a couple of hours. The last thing he remembered was stripping down and climbing onto the bed to wait for Stuart to come give him a massage.

"You're awake." Stuart's voice from the doorway startled him.

"Sorry. I was more tired than I realized."

"You fell asleep before I even got up here. I used the time to do some work, since we'll be at the hospital tomorrow."

"If you're busy, you don't have to come—"

"Don't be an asshole, Sergei," Stuart snapped. "Of course I'll be there to support you. We said I love you, and that means something to me."

"Sorry. I didn't mean to upset you. It means something to me too. I would love for you to come with me."

Stuart stared at him for a moment, obviously judging his sincerity, before he gave him a quick nod.

"Now that that's settled, how about the massage I promised you? I considered giving you one while you slept to help you sleep better, but the idea felt kind of skeevy to me."

"Skeevy?"

"You know, creepy, weird, stalkerish."

"Sometimes I wonder if we speak the same English language. Do you find those words in the romance novels you read?" That had been a surprise for Sergei. He'd thought Stuart only read comics and things for work. Sergei had picked up Stuart's Kindle one day when he'd left the room and found himself reading a sex scene between two male characters. Stuart had blushed so beautifully when he'd realized Sergei had seen it that Sergei gave him a hard time about it whenever he could.

Stuart gave him a haughty stare. "I'll have you know that I learn all sorts of things in my romance books. Some of them are even appropriate for talking about in public. I do believe you would probably enjoy some of the other things I've learned." Stuart moved his eyebrows up and down in an exaggerated manner, making Sergei laugh.

"Yes, *kotik*. Come show me some of those things you learned about." Sergei raised his hand, palm up, in invitation for Stuart to join him on the bed. Stuart took his hand and gave him a gentle kiss.

"Roll over onto your stomach. I still owe you that massage."

Sergei did as he'd been instructed, rolling over and putting his head on one of the pillows, his arms down by his sides. Stuart pulled the blankets and top sheet down to the end of the bed then grabbed some lotion from the bedside table. Sergei heard the bottle being opened and Stuart rubbing his hands together, obviously to warm the lotion a little before he started with the bottom of his right foot.

Stuart made his way slowly up his right leg, pausing every now then to add more cream to his hands. He stopped right at the edge of his butt before starting again at the bottom of his left foot. Sergei groaned. This was wonderful torture. This time when Stuart got to the top of the leg, he switched to Sergei's right hand, working his way up to his shoulder, then from Sergei's left hand to his shoulder.

Sergei watched through slitted eyes as Stuart stripped then climbed onto the bed and straddled him, so he was sitting just below his ass. He leaned forward and pressed his chest to Sergei's back to give him a gentle kiss before sitting back up, refreshing the lotion on his hands and starting to work on his neck and shoulders.

By the time Stuart had made his way all the way down to his ass again, Sergei couldn't decide whether to melt into a pile of goo or beg Stuart to fuck him. Reaching underneath himself, he adjusted his hardened cock, which was stuck at an awkward angle.

"Uh-uh. Hands off. That's mine."

Sergei moaned. "Then do something with it."

"All in good time." Stuart refreshed the lotion again before going to work on the muscles in his ass.

Sergei tried to spread his legs apart but found himself trapped by Stuart's legs on either side of his thighs. "Please, *kotik*."

Stuart pressed himself forward and ground his cock multiple times into the crease of Sergei's ass. "Fuck." Stuart moaned as he pushed up and back so that he was kneeling again, straddling Sergei's legs. Stuart forced one of his knees between them in a silent bid to allow him room, which he quickly did.

"Yes, please." Sergei was whining and he didn't care. He needed. It had been a while since Stuart had taken him. He craved it, something he'd never done with anyone else. He heard the lotion bottle open again then felt Stuart's finger at his hole. He focused on relaxing and letting Stuart in. One finger became two, then three. Sergei found himself pushing back on them, trying to get him deeper. He gasped when Stuart brushed his prostate, which he was obviously doing to drive Sergei out of his mind. "Please. Take me. I'm ready."

Sergei was both relieved and distressed when Stuart removed his fingers from his hole — relieved because it meant Stuart's cock would be in him soon and distressed because he was so very empty. Luckily, he didn't have to wait long. He heard the sound of a condom being opened then there was a pause before Stuart laid himself out over Sergei's back and pressed the head of his cock to Sergei's entrance.

Stuart slid in with one long, slow glide, not stopping until he was in as far as he could go. Stuart then put his legs on either side of Sergei's and pressed them back together before starting gentle rolling thrusts in and out. This position made it impossibly tight, but Sergei reveled in the feeling of fullness. He especially enjoyed it when Stuart shifted his hips so his boyfriend's cockhead was pressing into his prostate with every thrust. His position didn't allow him to stroke his own cock, but between what Stuart was doing and the rubbing of his cock on the sheets below him, he wasn't going to last long. It must have felt good to Stuart too, because he sped up and started babbling.

"Come on, Sergei. You have to come first."

A particularly hard thrust had Sergei putting his hands over his head on the headboard so he could get more leverage to push back. Stuart ground his hips against Sergei's ass and followed it up with three rapid thrusts, which sent Sergei over the edge with a shout. Stuart's long moan followed, and Sergei enjoyed the feel of Stuart emptying into the condom.

"We really need to get tested so we can go bare," Sergei mumbled, too sated to care that he was lying in the wet spot.

"Well, we can talk about it when you don't sound drunk."

Sergei lifted his head to look over his shoulder at Stuart. "You'd want to?"

"If we're serious and we're exclusive? Yeah, I'd want to."

Sergei dropped his head back to the pillow with a pleased grumble. "I've never gone bare before. I can't wait."

Stuart gently disengaged before his warmth disappeared from Sergei's back and he heard Stuart get off the bed and head in the direction of the bathroom. The water turned on and off a couple of times before Stuart returned and started cleaning the lotion and lube from the condom off his well-used hole. Stuart grabbed Sergei by the shoulder and gently rolled him over before cleaning off his front and taking a few swipes at the mess on the bed.

"We're going to have to change these sheets before tonight."

Sergei couldn't bring himself to care. "In a few minutes... Come here, *kotik*. Let me hold you." Stuart tossed the washcloth into the clothes hamper then climbed into bed, grabbing the covers on the way. Stuart settled with his head on Sergei's chest with a moan.

"You are so comfy."

"I'm glad you think so, *kotik*."

They lay in silence for a few minutes until Stuart broke it. "Were you serious about wanting to go bare?"

"Very serious. I can ask my doctor about it when he is running the other tests for me."

"I actually have a physical scheduled for next week. Bloodwork is on Tuesday. It's part of the bloodwork panel that my doctor always runs."

"Good." Sergei tightened his arms around Stuart for a moment before bending to kiss the top of his head. "I'm so glad I found you."

Sergei's stomach suddenly grumbled loudly, making Stuart snicker. "Hungry, babe?"

Sergei thought about it a moment. "Starving, for some reason."

"It's been a while since lunch. Let's head downstairs and see what I have. We'll eat then come back to bed."

"I'm not really tired right now."

"Who said anything about sleeping?"

"I like the way you think, Stuart." He was surprised when his boyfriend's head whipped around and he saw a shocked look. "What?"

"You called me by my name. You don't usually do that. It surprised me, is all. Never mind. Let's go eat."

* * * *

Walking back into the hospital the next day, Sergei was surprised by the number of people rushing around. There was a significant increase from the day before. He and Stuart weaved their way through the crowd and made their way to the elevator after checking in with security and getting visitor badges. Stuart was carrying coffee and Sergei was carrying the breakfast sandwiches and pastries they had picked up from their favorite café, so only Sergei had a hand free to press the button before stepping to the back of the elevator next to Stuart as more people loaded on. Sergei placed a hand around Stuart's waist to steady him when he was bumped by a mother with a stroller uttering frequent apologies to all around her. Luckily, they weren't on the elevator very long.

"Wow. I didn't think the coffees were actually going to make it for a minute there," Sergei said as he guided them down the hall toward Pyotr's room, since he'd never removed his arm from around Stuart.

"I know, right? That was close. Did you see the size of that stroller?"

"Did you see the size of the baby in the stroller? She was tiny."

"Right?" Stuart responded with a chuckle.

Stuart sobered as they approached the door to the room. "You can do this, babe. If you need to switch to Russian at any time, feel free. I know it's hard for Katia. If it's something I need to know, you can tell me later. Okay? I'm here for you."

Sergei pressed a quick kiss to Stuart's cheek before straightening, putting on what his family called his 'game face' and walking into the room.

"Good morning, Pyotr. Good morning, Katia. I hope you slept well. We've brought breakfast and coffee as promised."

Three heads turned toward them as they walked in — Pyotr and Katia and a medical professional.

"Ah, Sergei, you made it. I was just talking with the surgeon who is doing the procedure today. Doctor, this is my son Sergei. You can speak freely in front of him."

"Sounds good. I'm Doctor Carmichael." The doctor extended his hand in greeting and Sergei stepped forward to take it.

"Sergei Barinov."

A look of surprise crossed the doctor's face before he schooled it to a professional mask. "Mr. Barinov, it is a pleasure to meet you. You've done a lot of good things for the community. I did not realize Mr. Popomov was your father."

"Sean Hamilton is my father," Sergei said grimly. "Pyotr was simply my sperm donor." Sergei only spared a glance for Katia and Pyotr when his sister gasped. He saw shocked horror on her face and sadness on Pyotr's but he couldn't find it in him to care. He turned his attention back to the doctor. "Now…what will happen today?"

To the doctor's credit, he pulled himself together quickly. "We'll be wheeling your father down to the operating room shortly. You all can move down to the surgery waiting room then. One person will be allowed into the recovery room once he awakens."

"That will be me," Katia interjected.

"Okay. Well, the nurse will come to get you when it's time. I'll come tell you how it went after surgery. I've performed this operation many times and do not anticipate that there will be any problems. Other than this issue, Mr. Popomov seems to be in good shape. Are there any questions?" He waited an appropriate few moments and received no response. "All right then. I'll see you in a bit. As I said, they will be in shortly to take him to prep."

The doctor gave Sergei another long look before he turned and left the room. Sergei turned to find Katia giving him a disapproving look. "What?"

"We will discuss it later."

Sergei shrugged. He really didn't care what had upset her so much, but he would listen. Stuart's hand sliding into his startled him. He glanced at his boyfriend to find Stuart shaking his head at him. "What?"

"Be nice."

Sergei was totally confused. "I *am* being nice."

"Telling the doctor that Pyotr was only your sperm donor was nice?"

"I didn't tell him he was an adulterous, opportunistic jerk who knocked up a fifteen-year-old student and stole her research. I consider calling him my sperm donor being nice."

Katia turned and looked at Pyotr in shock. "You did not say she was so young."

Pyotr shrugged, looking suddenly tired and old. "It was a long time ago in a different time. Fifteen was not very young in Russia then. Daria was and still is, in all likelihood, an old soul. She was never really allowed to be a child, due to the number of children in her family and her absolute brilliance. She is a shining star."

A nurse and a couple of orderlies came into the room in a flurry of activity, asking questions and loading Pyotr onto the gurney. Katia leaned down and gave her father a kiss before the orderlies rolled Pyotr out of the room.

The nurse turned to the three of them. "Your father is in good hands. Doctor Carmichael is one of the best in the country. If you'll follow me, I'll take you to the surgical waiting room."

"Thank you, ma'am," Stuart responded for them all. "How is your day going? Have you been super busy?"

Sergei tuned out the conversation as he and Katia followed in their wake. He felt Katia shooting looks at him as they walked but didn't want to start a conversation with her in the hallway. Reaching the entrance to a place with 'Waiting Room' on a sign above it, he indicated for Katia to enter first. It wasn't exactly cozy, although he thought maybe cozy and calming was what they were going for, but it wasn't the worst waiting room he had ever been in. The one at the orthopedic walk-in he had been in recently with Sasha came to mind. There were five other people there, but no one paid any attention to them after first looking up to make sure it wasn't someone they knew or needed to talk with.

Sergei pointed to an empty section of the room. "Let's sit over there. Then we can talk." He strode over to the two-seater in the corner and pulled Stuart down next to him, forcing Katia to sit on the chair on the opposite side of the little corner end table.

Sergei rested his lower arms on his thighs and laced his fingers together. "Go ahead and say whatever it is you feel you need to say. If it would be easier, Stuart has said it's okay for us to talk in Russian, but know that I will be telling him what we talk about later."

Katia darted a look in Stuart's direction and Sergei felt more than saw him nod at Katia in encouragement before he placed a hand on Sergei's thigh in a show of support that Sergei truly appreciated as Katia started speaking to him in Russian.

"I didn't know your mother was so young. Father said he had an affair and a son, but he never said she was one of his students or that she was so young."

Sergei scoffed. *"I'm guessing he also didn't tell you that he stole her work and presented it as his own?"*

Katia looked horrified for a moment. *"No. He didn't say anything about stealing her work."* She paused as if to gather her thoughts. *"I didn't know of you until after my mother died. He told us about the two of you and how you had moved to the United States. He told us how he missed your growing up."*

Sergei quirked an eyebrow at her.

"What? Why do you look at me like that?" Katia was obviously perplexed by his attitude.

"He wouldn't even let Mama put his name on the birth certificate and he never spent any time with me at all. Am I supposed to feel bad for him?"

"No, I suppose not." Long pause. *"He really didn't let them put his name on the birth certificate?"*

"No. He didn't want anyone to find out that he'd had sex with a student. He said it would ruin his reputation."

"Do you have any other siblings?"

"Yes, I have a sister, Natasha, who is twenty-one and a brother, Alexander, who is sixteen."

"Wow. You have a brother just barely older than my children."

"Yes, I suppose that's true."

"And you're gay? Stuart is your boyfriend?"

"Bi, but yes, Stuart is my boyfriend."

There was an even longer pause before she almost whispered, *"I think my son might be gay. It is not a good thing to be gay in Russia. I worry for him."* Another pause. *"I know I don't have the right to ask you, but if it becomes necessary, will you help me to get him out of Russia? Perhaps he can come to school here and you could watch out for him."*

Sergei sat back in his chair in stunned silence for a moment, before answering her. *"Your son is an innocent in all this. If he needs my help, I will do all I can for him. He should not be punished for being gay."*

Katia deflated like all her strings had been cut. *"I do not want to send my son so far away, but I want him to be safe. I doubt he can ever be gay and safe in Russia."*

Sergei looked at her with suspicion. *"Is that why you came with Pyotr on this trip?"*

"Yes. Now it turns out it was a good thing I did, for all this." Katia waved a hand around at the waiting room. *"But Papa and I had a conversation about the possibility that my son could be gay, and he suggested I come meet you and maybe you could help when the time was right."*

"What does your husband think of all this?"

"He doesn't know. He's the one I worry about the most if it's discovered. He's not a nice man. He was once upon a time, but he has become more and more intolerant as time has gone on."

"I can help you too, if ever there comes a time you need to get away."

A sad smile crossed Katia's face. *"I appreciate that, more than I can say. I will let you know. For now, I think we've excluded your boyfriend enough."*

Sergei shot a look in Stuart's direction to find him looking at his phone. He must have sensed them looking at him, because he turned his head and met Sergei's gaze.

"Did you say something to me?"

"No, *kotik*. We were just saying we've excluded you enough."

"It's okay, babe. I'm reading through work emails. I'm not bothered. I'm here to support you." Stuart squeezed his hand around Sergei's thigh. "Carry on."

Laughing, he turned back to Katia to find her watching them with a weird look on her face. "What?"

"You really do care for one another."

"Yes, we do."

"That's nice."

"Does your husband not care for you in the same way?"

Katia hesitated before she responded. "No, not like he loves me. He acts more like I'm a responsibility he no longer wishes to have."

"I'm so sorry to hear that."

"Me too," Stuart added. "You shouldn't feel that way."

"I know. My children will be out of the house soon. I am trying to get things in order in the remaining time. It was one of the things Sergei and I were discussing."

"I'll fill you in later," Sergei said as he put his hand over the hand on his thigh and laced their fingers together. "For now, let's eat the breakfast we brought and try to relax as we wait."

Chapter Thirteen

Stuart looked around at all their friends as they gathered for Thanksgiving at Lee and Saul's apartment. He had a lot to be thankful for this year. Pyotr had made it through surgery without any issues and had returned to Russia with Katia. Sergei had been tested and found he didn't have the heart defect, so that was a major relief. The doctor had cautioned that if Sergei fathered any children in the future, they would need to be tested as well, but that was easy enough to do.

"You're looking quite happy, my friend." Lee's comment startled him out of his introspection.

"I was just thinking that I have a lot to be thankful for this year—having somewhere to go for both holidays being one of them. Thank you so much for inviting me."

"You know you're welcome here anytime," Lee said while giving Stuart a side-armed hug. "Even if the event was at Mama's, you could still come. You're family."

Stuart felt himself well up for a moment, but he was so happy that there was no need for tears. "Thanks, dude. I appreciate it. Truly."

"How are things going with the big guy and his family?" Lee asked with a head tilt toward Sergei, who was across the room having some sort of discussion with Saul in the kitchen that involved lots of hand waving.

"They're going good" — Stuart's grin widened then fell — "other than his sister and her boyfriend, that is. Natasha still hates me." Stuart shrugged. "There's not much I can do about it other than keep trying to talk to her. Sergei says she'll come around and that he's never seen her act this way, but we'll see. Speaking of Sergei's family, how is Nikolai doing at the garage?"

"The man is a miracle worker. The front desk has never been so organized, and it gives him a place to work on his dissertation in between customers. It's a win-win for everyone."

"Good to hear. I've really enjoyed talking to Nikolai. He's so different from Sergei that it's hard to imagine they're even cousins."

"I know, right? He should be here soon. He was making a couple of pies to bring. He called to say he was running a bit late."

"That's great."

"Yep. I'm really not sure we needed more food, though," Lee said with a wave in the direction of the already-full countertops.

"I think I said the same thing at my birthday, but as someone said, I think you'll be surprised how little is left with this crowd."

"True. So, what's going on with Nikolai and Brandon?"

"You've noticed it too?"

"It's hard not to. Nikolai becomes the most uncoordinated, ditzy spaz whenever Brandon is around."

"Right?" Stuart couldn't stop his chuckle. "It should be interesting to see how that plays out."

"Agreed. I can't wait. You going to the theater tomorrow to work on the sets some more?"

"Yeah. Sergei has a conference call with some people in Europe, which means I can go between nine and, like...two."

"Saul has a class tomorrow morning, so I can meet you there."

"Sounds good. We only have one backdrop to finish, so hopefully we won't have to be there that long if we work together."

"Show's in what, two weeks?"

"A little over, yeah. The shows run from December twelfth through the fifteenth. Sergei's family is coming to the final performance on Saturday evening, then we're all supposed to be going out to dinner at Puzzles. Natasha is supposed to be done with the semester then, so she can make it." Stuart hoped the eye roll communicated how excited he was about the fact Natasha would be joining the family celebration.

Lee chuckled. "Make sure you sit at the opposite end of the table from her and you should be fine. Remember... Don't make eye contact with wild animals."

"Who's a wild animal?" Nikolai asked as he bounded up to the two of them.

"Nikolai! I didn't see you come in." Lee patted him on the shoulder in greeting. "And we were talking about Natasha. I was telling Stuart not to make eye contact with Natasha when the family goes out to dinner after the play Saturday the fifteenth."

"Yeah. That's probably a great idea. That girl has lost her mind lately. I have no idea what her issue is. Aunt Daria has about had it with her. She really has it in for you, for some reason."

"As I told Lee, all I can do at this point is keep trying to talk to her and show her I'm not a bad guy. Adulting sucks sometimes."

"It really does." Nikolai nodded his head vigorously.

"You liking it at the garage, though?"

"Yeah. It's completely different from working at Sergei's company, but it lets me get work done on my dissertation and for clients. I never wanted to go into the big business side of things."

"I completely understand. I like working for myself."

An evil glint came into Nikolai's eyes. "So, tell me. What happened when Daria and Sean went to see Pyotr? Sergei will only say it was fine."

Stuart shrugged. "It *was* fine. Weird, but fine. Everyone was eerily polite. Pyotr kept trying to engage Daria in conversation about what she's working on and hinting that he would love to work with her again."

"How was that weird?"

"Sergei didn't really pick up on it, since it's his mom and all, but there was this weird sexual tension between them. Pyotr really laid on the charm and flirting. I can see why she fell for him, especially since she was so young."

"Really? How did Sean handle it?"

"He put his arm around Daria, pulled her up close to him and told Pyotr that she was busy enough already, being the head of her department and in high demand. Between work and her family, she really didn't have any time."

"Oh, I'm sure Aunt Daria was not happy with that."

"Nope. Sergei was looking at them all like 'what the hell is going on here?'. For a man who is so smart, he doesn't pick up social cues very well."

"I know, right?"

"And Daria was glaring at both of them like 'oh no you didn't', but she turned to Sean and patted his cheek and was all 'I can handle this, dear'. Sean's eyes got really big because he knew he was in trouble, but then I thought he was going to hyperventilate from how much she turned him on when she told Pyotr off. I have no idea what she said, because she switched to Russian for it, but Pyotr almost fainted and the nurse came rushing in because I guess his heart monitor was connected to something at the nurse's station and it was going nuts."

"OMG. What did everyone do?"

"Daria turned to the nurse and was like. *'I'm so sorry. He's my ex and I thought he was over me, but obviously I still do it for him'*, then she stepped forward so her back was to Sean and Sergei and said *'Pyotr, for your safety I need to leave. I won't be working on any projects with you now or in the future. Get well soon.'*, and she turned and sailed out of the room like a queen, leaving Sean there opening and closing his mouth like a fish before he said a quick goodbye and started chasing after her."

Nikolai clapped his hands together and laughed. "I wish I could have been a fly on the wall to witness that."

"It was awesome. Sergei was standing there looking very confused. I had to explain it to him after we left.

He was all"—Stuart deepened his voice in a poor imitation of Sergei's sexy baritone—"Oh no. My mom doesn't do sexual tension."

Lee and Nikolai roared with laughter, drawing the attention of everyone else in the room. Stuart looked up and found Sergei staring at him with a heat that made Stuart want to drag him off to a quiet room somewhere. He winked at Sergei and enjoyed the grin he got in return.

"Man, you two are sappy," Lee muttered while giving him a shoulder bump.

"Like you can talk. You and Saul are worse."

Nikolai looked at Stuart with wide eyes. "Right? I walked in on him and Saul making out in the breakroom yesterday. Lordy, talk about hot." Nikolai fanned his face with his hand.

The three men cracked up again, right before hearing a little girl yell Stuart's name. Stuart barely caught Sam when she jumped at him. He spun her in a circle and made her squeal.

"Don't drop me, Uncle Stu!"

"As if."

Sam looped her arms around Stuart's neck. "My laptop's not acting right. Can you look at it?"

"Sure thing. Where is it?"

Sam pointed toward the couch, where he could see the laptop sitting on the end table. He carried Sam over and set her down, picking up the laptop and putting it on his lap so he could take a look. It only took him a few moments to figure out the problem.

"It looks like you've picked up a virus, kiddo. What sites have you been on?"

When he didn't get a response, he looked over at Sam to find her looking at her shoes.

"Sam?"

"I didn't mean to," she whispered as a blush covered her face.

"Didn't mean to what, sweetie?" Stuart reached out and turned her face so he could see her eyes.

"Everyone at school was talking about this one website, but I typed it in wrong." Sam stopped there.

"I'm guessing you went to a site you weren't supposed to."

"There were all these naked people," Sam whispered again.

Oh, lord. Where did she go?

"Okay, Sam. I'll fix it and I'll put some controls on your computer so you can't go to one of those sites again accidentally. Is Claire's computer here too?"

Sam shook her head. "I just brought mine because Papa said you could fix it."

"And did you tell him why it was broken?"

Sam shook her head dejectedly and a tear tracked down her cheek. "I didn't mean to do it."

"Hey, sweetie, don't cry. These things happen to all of us. Let the adults help you so you don't accidentally see more than you're ready for, okay? And you know if you ever have any questions, there are plenty of people to talk to. Right?"

"Right."

"Okay. Then why don't you go get Kirk—I mean your papa—and have him meet me in the office and let's see if we can get this laptop straightened out."

Sam threw her arms around Stuart's neck and gave him a hug before running off in search of Kirk. Stuart scooped up the laptop and walked over to where Lee was still talking to Nikolai. "Lee, do you care if I borrow your office for a few minutes? Sam seems to have picked up a virus."

"She seemed pretty upset. Is she okay?"

Stuart lowered his voice so only Nikolai and Lee could hear him. "She typed in a website wrong and ended up somewhere she wasn't supposed to be. There were naked people."

"Oh wow," Nikolai giggled. "I remember the first time I accidentally did that. Of course, it wasn't so accidental the next time."

"Yeah. We've all been there. Go ahead and use the office. Dinner isn't for another hour. How long will it take you?"

"I'll probably set up a scan and let it run while we eat. I'm more concerned with setting up the parental controls and showing Kirk how to do it for Claire's computer too."

"Yeah. It's a weird world we live in now."

As he made his way to the office, Stuart spared a glance for Sergei, where he appeared to be arguing with Saul in the kitchen about the correct way to baste a turkey, of all things. It suddenly hit him. *I have a family – a real family where I'm always welcome and belong.* He had a place. People counted on him and included him. With a shake of his head, he continued to where he was needed to complete uncle duties, and tomorrow, he would help Saul's brother. His life was busier than ever, and he loved it.

Chapter Fourteen

Sergei sat in the audience with his family, waiting for the second act of Sasha's play to begin. He was in awe of all the sets, which by all accounts Lee and Stuart had mostly done by themselves. The trees looked almost real. It was amazing. He couldn't say he would be sad when the play was over, though.

Stuart had been very busy the last couple of weeks. Between Stuart's work responsibilities — where he was trying to get ahead so he could take a couple weeks off at the holidays — and the play, as well as Sergei's own work, they hadn't had much of a chance to see each other. They'd made an effort to talk to each other every day, but that wasn't nearly the same. He really needed to speak with Stuart about combining households. Then at least they would usually end up in the same place at night. Perhaps Stuart could even travel with him, if he could work remotely.

His thoughts were interrupted by Stuart coming out on stage, carrying a guitar for some reason. He raised his hands to get the crowd's attention and to get them to quiet down.

"We're having a bit of a technical glitch, so it will be a few more minutes before we can get started on the second half of our production of *Into the Woods*. I've been sent out here to distract you from the delay with hints of what our next show is going to be. I've also been asked to tell you that auditions will be held on January fifteenth." Stuart strummed the guitar for a few moments before beginning to sing about having a brain.

Stuart's fantastic tenor sent shivers down Sergei's spine as he heard excited whispers about *The Wizard of Oz* being the next play. But mostly he tuned them out as he watched his boyfriend play and sing to the crowd. To think, the man thought he was boring and nondescript. He obviously didn't realize the way his face lit up when he was happy, the way his body was designed to be absolutely perfect to drive him mad or how the sound of his voice could make him shiver.

Sergei's mother leaned over and handed him a tissue and he tore his gaze away from his boyfriend to look at her in question. "You're drooling."

"Ha-ha, Mama. You think you're so funny."

"I know I am. I'm happy to see you finally in love. I was worried it wouldn't happen."

"I don't think I had a choice, Mama. He's meant to be mine."

His mother leaned her head against his shoulder and hummed in agreement—or happiness, he couldn't say which. It didn't really matter, though, as he turned his attention back to his boyfriend when he finished up the song with a flourish. He looked off stage for a moment before he turned his attention back to the crowd.

"Okay then. It appears we are ready to continue our journey *Into the Woods*. Maestro." With a wave in the direction of the small orchestra, Stuart bowed and made his way off the stage.

The next hour flew by as Sergei was once again entranced by the quality of the work of the small theater company. After the show and the numerous curtain calls, Sergei made his way with the rest of the family to congratulate Sasha.

"Great job, Sasha. You've really improved."

Sasha's face lit up. "Yeah. Stuart has been working with me. It's been great. I'm glad you started dating him."

"I'm so glad my dating has improved your life," Sergei replied dryly.

"Well, it hasn't improved mine. I think you should dump him," Natasha interjected with a flip of her hair.

Before Sergei could figure out how to respond, his mother jumped in. "No one asked your opinion, Natasha, and we will be discussing your attitude tomorrow. For tonight, let's enjoy a nice family dinner out. Reggie is meeting us at Puzzles, correct?"

Natasha shot everyone a dirty look and crossed her arms over her chest before responding. "Yes. He's heading over as soon as I call him. How much longer are you going to be?" The last question was directed at Sasha.

"I need to wash off the make-up really quick and get into my street clothes, so maybe fifteen minutes? If you guys want to head over and get a table, I can catch a ride with Stuart."

"Which means I'll wait too, as I'm Stuart's ride tonight," Sergei said.

Sean clapped Sergei on the shoulder. "Sounds like a plan. We'll go get a table and you wait for Stuart and Sasha. Great job tonight, son." Sean enveloped Sasha in a hug and clapped him on the back before releasing him so his mother could hug him. "We'll see you at the restaurant in a little bit. Come on, Natasha. We can chat on the ride to the restaurant."

Natasha set her face in a mutinous expression and stomped her way to the door, resembling a tantrum-throwing two-year-old more than the twenty-one-year-old adult she was supposed to be.

"Come on, Sergei. Let me go get changed and we can grab Stuart. I'm starving."

"You're always starving," Sergei mumbled, but he dutifully followed Sasha backstage, where he found Stuart in the middle of a group of people. Lee and Saul were there, as well as a young man Sergei didn't know who was hanging on Stuart's arm and staring at him like he'd hung the moon and stars. "Who's that?" Sergei asked, pointing at the made-up, skintight-jeans-and-high-heels-wearing youngster.

"Who?" Sasha looked in the direction Sergei was pointing and snorted a laugh. "Oh, that's Patrick's older brother, home from college for winter break. He's been trying to get Stuart's attention all week. It's been hysterical to watch."

"Interesting. Stuart hasn't mentioned him." Sergei couldn't quite keep the growl out of his voice.

"Because Stuart hasn't realized he's flirting with him or that he even exists, really. He's been so busy with the play. I mean, we've all told him he doesn't have a chance and that Stuart has a boyfriend, but the guy is just not buying a clue."

"Well" — Sergei arched a brow at Sasha — "let's see if we can get him one."

Sergei made his way to Stuart's side, making sure to position himself between his boyfriend and the little twink, poacher wannabe. Lee chuckled but Sergei ignored him. "Hey, babe." He framed Stuart's face with his hands and pulled him in for a kiss. Stuart looked at him quizzically when he pulled back. "I loved your singing. That was fantastic. You'll have to give me a private show later." He leaned back in for another peck to the sound of Lee, Saul and Sasha laughing, but more importantly, the sigh and muttered, "Figures," from the man behind him.

Stuart still looked confused until Sasha spoke up. "We tried to tell you he was taken, man. You should've believed us."

"He's not wearing a ring. That means he's still up for grabs."

Sasha laughed. "Do you see my brother? If my brother's his type, do you really think you stand a chance?"

"From what I heard, your brother is everyone's type. I'll just wait until he gets bored and moves on, then I'll be here to console him."

Sergei didn't like the look of concern that crossed Stuart's face at the mention of him getting bored, but before he could comment, Stuart leaned around him and looked at the young man behind him. "You do know I can hear you, right?"

"Oh. Oh…sorry. I didn't mean anything by it. Um, I need to go find my family."

The man left, the click of his heels loud in the sudden silence.

"Wow. A show after the show—and here I am without any popcorn," Saul drawled.

"You two didn't have to embarrass him," Stuart scolded both Sergei and Sasha. "I didn't even realize he had a crush."

"Man, we've all been telling him for days that you're taken, to give it up and that you didn't even notice him in a romantic way. He wouldn't listen."

Stuart shook his head at the two of them. "Anyway, go get into your street clothes so we can head to dinner with your family. I don't want you to be late to the after-party. It starts at ten, right?"

"Right."

"Then shoo. Let's get moving. We're waiting on you, dude, and I'm starving."

"Going. Going."

"And you, sir. Knock it off. I am happy to take your kisses at any time, but there is no need for the chest thumping. Geez," Stuart told Sergei.

"I am honestly shocked at my own behavior. I've never felt the need to stake my claim before."

Lee clapped Sergei on the back. "Welcome to the love club. It makes us all do weird things."

"Subject change." Stuart turned to look at Lee. "Are you coming tomorrow morning to help with set breakdown?"

"Yep. Saul said he'd come help too. It shouldn't take long."

"Yeah, and the good news is they can reuse some of the trees for *Wizard of Oz*," Stuart said.

"Oh, I didn't even think of that." Lee's eyes lit up with excitement. "You helping out with it?"

Stuart shrugged. "I'm not sure yet. I need a break right now. It's been a lot."

"Yeah. I get that for sure. Let me know."

Sasha came to join all of them. "Ready?"

"Yep. Let's go. See you tomorrow, Lee. Maybe we can do lunch after?"

"Sounds good. Sergei, are you coming tomorrow?"

"Sure. Why not."

"Great. We'll see you in the morning then."

"Come on, Neanderthal. Let's go." Stuart grabbed his hand and led him toward the doors.

Sasha talked about the show the entire ride to the restaurant, requiring very little response from either of them, for which Sergei was thankful. He was still stuck on his strange behavior. It had been like dropping a building on a housefly. Stuart hadn't even been paying any attention to the young man.

Stuart whispered to him, "Let it go."

"What?"

"It's okay. We're new. It'll settle."

"Yeah?"

"Yeah. We're still figuring things out, but know this"—Stuart paused to squeeze Sergei's thigh—"I'm yours, well and truly. I'm not going anywhere."

Something settled in Sergei. "I'm yours too and you're stuck with me." Grabbing Stuart's hand, he raised it to his lips and gave it a kiss.

Stuart gently extracted his hand. "Later, Neanderthal."

Walking into the restaurant a few minutes later, Sergei looked around for his family. Discovering that they were at a table to the back, he weaved his way through the tables to join them. Greeting everyone, he sat at one of the three empty spots with Stuart taking the seat beside him.

They had given their drink orders when Reggie suddenly spoke up. "Hey, I see a friend of mine at the bar. I'll be right back. Anyone want anything?" He barely waited for anyone's responses before he was up and away from the table.

Stuart cleared his throat as he also stood. "I'm actually going to hit the little gents' room. I'll be right back too."

Sergei turned to Sean. "What did you think of the play?"

"I was really impressed with the theater company, as well as the play itself. This was the first production Sasha's done with them. Your boyfriend and his friend did an amazing job on the sets for the show."

"They really did, didn't they? I was really impressed."

Sasha joined the conversation. "I can't wait for auditions for *Wizard of Oz*. It's a mixed adults and kids show, so it should be fun. The director is trying to get Stuart to audition for the part of the Scarecrow."

"He did amazing tonight, that's for sure," Daria quickly added.

"Eh. He was okay," Natasha said with a head toss.

"What is your deal, Natasha? Stuart has been nothing but nice to you."

"Things were fine before he came into your life. He's changing everything!"

"When you find your heart, that's what happens!"

A disturbance from the direction of the restrooms had them all looking over there. Sergei was surprised to see some of the bouncers rushing in that direction.

"Stay here," he directed everyone as he made his way over to see what was going on. "What's up,

Steve?" He addressed his restaurant manager as he made it to the door.

"From what I understand, Stuart witnessed a drug exchange in the restroom. The cops are already in there." Sergei sensed movement out of the corner of his eye and turned his head to watch an officer exit the men's restroom and make his way through the crowd to where Sergei and Steve were standing.

"Mr. Barinov," one of the officers addressed him. "Steve."

"You guys got here quickly."

"We were actually outside. We have an undercover officer who has been trying to collect evidence on a local drug dealer. He walked in at the tail end of the drug exchange. Your boyfriend witnessed everything and distracted them enough so that they didn't hear him come in."

Natasha appeared at Sergei's shoulder. "Have you seen Reggie? I can't find him anywhere."

A sense of dread moved through Sergei. "Officer, who was the drug dealer?"

"A guy by the name of Jacob Jones."

Sergei closed his eyes for a moment, hating to ask the next question. "And the buyer?"

"A young man by the name of Reginald Worthington."

"No! You're lying. Reggie doesn't do drugs. Stuart's in there, too, isn't he? He probably planted the drugs."

Right then, Reggie and another young man — who must be Jacob Jones — were brought out of the restroom in handcuffs.

Reggie yelled to Natasha as he was being led away. "Baby, I didn't do anything. Stuart tried to hit on me in the restroom. Don't believe him, baby. You know I don't do drugs."

Reggie continued to yell about his innocence the whole time he was led out of the restaurant. Natasha tried to follow him but Sergei grabbed hold of her and wouldn't let her.

"Let me go. I have to help him."

Stuart came out of the restroom next and Natasha switched her focus to him. She jerked free of Sergei and flew at Stuart, slapping him across the face then pounding on his chest. Stuart grabbed a hold of her upper arms.

"You did this! This is all your fault! You are a disgusting, horrible human being. I hope you die a horrible death!"

"Stuart, don't hurt her!" Sergei distantly registered the look of hurt on Stuart's face before he reached out, grabbed hold of Natasha again and pulled her away from him. He put his arms around her and tried to get her to calm down. "Natasha, you need to stop. This isn't helping. Natasha, *stop*. We'll figure out what's going on. Calm down *now*!"

The rest of Sergei's family joined him, and he was able to hand Natasha off to his mother after a few more minutes. When he looked up to search for Stuart, he was gone. He turned to the uniformed police officer, who was still standing next to them.

"Where did Stuart go?"

"You mean after you totally ignored him in favor of comforting your out-of-control sister instead of checking on him after she attacked him?" He paused for a moment before continuing. "I'm not at liberty to say, sir."

Sergei was stunned. "That's not what happened."

The officer raised a single eyebrow at him. "Whatever you say, sir."

Sasha interrupted. "I talked to him. They took him to take his statement." Sergei was surprised to see the look of disappointment Sasha leveled at him. "He asked me to give you this." Sasha paused to hand Sergei his house key. "He said you could drop his key off at the garage. He'll get it later."

"What?"

"Bro, you defended the psycho instead of your boyfriend. How did you think he was going to feel about that?"

"I wanted her to stop hitting him."

"Yeah, by telling *him* not to hurt her. Then you calmed her down instead of handing her off and going to him. You didn't even notice that he'd left." Sasha shook his head at him before turning and walking away.

Sergei stared down at the key for a moment before swallowing hard and putting it in his pocket. He would fix this. Right now, he had to figure out what the hell had just happened. He hardened his heart and put his game face on, ready to get to work.

Chapter Fifteen

Stuart sat in the police station for the third straight hour, giving his statement again and again. His stomach grumbled noisily, reminding him that he hadn't had any dinner yet. Since he'd been too keyed up about the production, he hadn't had much to eat throughout the day, and he was paying for it now. The officer's head came up when Stuart's stomach growled loud enough that he'd obviously heard it from the other side of the table.

"Hungry?"

"Starving, actually."

"Well, I just need you to read through the statement and sign it, and we can let you go. I must caution you, though, that this is an ongoing investigation, so we need to ask you not be in contact with the Hamiltons or Mr. Barinov until we say it's okay."

Stuart swallowed hard. "Is that at their request?"

"No, ours. I understand Mr. Barinov has been told the same thing and he is not happy about it. By the way, here. I was asked to give this back to you." The officer reached into his pocket and handed Stuart the key he had impulsively taken off his keychain and given to Sasha to return to Sergei. He'd been so pissed. It was perhaps not the most mature reaction, though. Was it too much to ask to be first in someone's life?

Stuart realized when the officer cleared his throat that he had been sitting and staring at the key instead of reaching for it. He quickly raised his hand and took the key back. He wasn't sure what was going to happen in the future, but it gave him a smidgen of hope to know that Sergei still wanted him to have it. Now Stuart had to decide what he was going to do with the information.

Stuart cleared his throat before responding. "Thank you."

"You know, he was really upset when his brother gave it to him."

"Yeah?" Stuart couldn't help feeling a little more hopeful and it showed in his voice when he asked the question.

"Yeah."

"Oh."

"Yeah, oh. Here's the statement. Read through it then sign on that bottom line and I can let you go."

"Thank you."

Stuart quickly read everything through, his mind going back to what he had witnessed.

He heard the door open while he was buckling his belt and getting ready to exit the bathroom stall. Vaguely he thought it was weird that the guy was pacing back and forth in front of the sink, but what did he know? The door opened a second time and he heard a voice call out.

"Yo, Reggie."

Reggie? What was Reggie doing meeting with someone in the restroom?

"Hey, Jacob." Stuart heard their hands slapping together in some sort of greeting. "You got what I need?"

"Yep. More of the liquid Ritalin. Fifty bucks."

"Hear ya go."

"Still effective?"

"Oh yeah. I put it in her tea in the morning and she barely eats. She's lost weight. She's lost all the baby fat and looks fantastic. She credits my special tea for helping her focus. It's a total win-win. She's not sleeping at night, though. What do you have that I can give her at night?"

Stuart had heard enough. He pulled open the stall door, watching Reggie's eyes get big as he realized he'd been caught. Reggie started to make a break for it and Stuart made a move to grab both young men, only to be stopped by a man who had appeared at the door to the restroom. He flashed his badge at everyone and drew his gun before he stepped farther into the room. "Police. I'm Officer Parker. Let me see your hands. Well, well. What do we have here?"

"I overheard this guy selling liquid Ritalin to Reggie here. He said he's been putting it in my boyfriend's sister's tea."

"Well then," the plain clothes officer said, "that gives me probable cause to search you both. Put your hands on the wall, gentlemen, and spread 'em."

Reggie shot Stuart a dirty look before he complied with the officer. The officer yelled in the direction of the door, "Jackson!" One of the bouncers poked his head in and looked at what was going on.

"Did you catch him in the act?"

"No, but a witness did. Keep everyone out, please. I've been trying to find who's been selling in the area." The officer stepped forward and searched them. He pulled multiple plastic packets and some small bottles out of Jacob's pockets and placed them in a pile on the floor before turning to Reggie *and searching him as well, pulling the small bottle he had purchased from Jacob out of his front pocket and laying it on the floor to create a separate pile. "Well, gentlemen, you are both under arrest for possession of a controlled substance. Jacob, you get the bonus charge of intent to distribute and whatever else I can come up with." He read them their rights as he cuffed both of them. Once he was done, he made them turn and sit on the floor with their backs to the wall. He pulled out his phone and called for backup before he shot a glance in Stuart's direction. "Who are you?"*

"I'm Stuart Woods. Reggie and I are both here with the Hamilton family for dinner." He pointed at Reggie to indicate who he was talking about. "Reggie is dating Natasha Hamilton and I'm dating her brother Sergei Barinov."

Stuart watched the officer's eyes widen momentarily in shock before they narrowed at him in assessment.

"Half-brother," Reggie interjected with a snarl.

"The half means nothing to Sergei. She's his sister," Stuart snarled back.

"Wait!" Jacob whipped his head to the side to glare at Reggie. "Your girlfriend is Sergei Barinov's sister? You never told me that!"

"What difference does it make?"

"Do you not know who Sergei is?"

"Some wannabe." Reggie answered with a shrug, but a hint of doubt showed in his eyes for the first time.

"Dude, he owns like a bunch of restaurants and other businesses here and other places like New York City. He's the real deal. He has his hands in so many pies around here that it's not funny. Oh man… Oh man, I'm so dead." Jacob thunked his head against the wall behind him.

The officer smirked at Stuart before continuing his questions. "And what do you do, Mr. Woods?"

"I'm a graphic artist and website designer. I own Woods Graphic Design."

"And how long have you been dating Mr. Barinov?"

"Three months or so. I'm not sure that's relevant, though."

"It's not really. HR says I need to work on my people skills. I was trying to practice what they taught me in the class they sent me to about how to talk to witnesses."

Stuart couldn't help the snicker that escaped. "You need a little work still."

"Oh well. Practice makes perfect." He shrugged before turning serious again. "Walk me through what you heard and saw here."

Stuart told him everything. A disturbance at the door as he finished heralded the arrival of a couple of uniformed officers.

After reading through the report, Stuart signed the document, trying hard not to think about what happened next before handing it back to the officer. "Is that it?"

"Yep. That's it for now. You're free to go. As I said, please, no contact with the Hamiltons or Mr. Barinov for the time being. The investigation shouldn't take long."

"Okay," Stuart agreed with a sigh before standing and stretching his stiff muscles. "Now, I just have to figure out how I'm getting home. Sergei was my ride."

"That won't be a problem. Your friend Lee arrived about a half hour ago. He's waiting for you outside."

"Really? That's fantastic news." Stuart turned to leave but was stopped by the officer.

"Oh wait, one last thing. Take Officer Parker's and my cards. Call us if you have any questions or remember anything else."

"I will. Thank you. Have a nice night. Please keep me posted." After taking the cards, Stuart spun on his heel and went outside, where Lee was leaning against the hood of his car in the parking lot. Stuart swallowed the emotion trying to choke him and made his way over to his friend. He tried for a smile and found it beyond him. Lee reached out and pulled him into a tight hug before he could figure out what to say. Stuart dropped his head down on Lee's shoulder and attempted to get his emotions under control. Once he'd managed it, he gave Lee a shaky smile.

"Thanks for coming to get me."

"Yeah. Sergei called. He's really upset that they won't let him talk to you right now." Lee paused for a moment. "He told me what happened. He wanted me to tell you he didn't mean it like that. He wouldn't have held it against you if you'd defended yourself against Natasha, but he knew you would hate yourself if you did."

Stuart thought about it for a minute before he nodded his head. "He's probably right. I mean, I'm telling myself it's the drugs making her act so ugly, but it's a struggle right now."

"Right? Come on. Let's get you home." Lee didn't speak again until they were both settled into the car and Lee had put it in Drive. "You better call Paul too. He's going to be pissed if you don't tell him about all this right away."

With a heartfelt sigh that seemed to come from his toes, Stuart pulled out his phone, found Paul's number and hit connect. Paul answered on the third ring.

"What's wrong? You never call me this late."

"I'm going to put you on speaker. Lee's here too. He's driving me home from the police station. I'll tell you both my side of what happened at the same time."

"Police station? *What*?" Paul's voice was loud and echoed through the car.

Stuart went through the whole thing again, leaving nothing out.

"That bastard!"

"Which bastard are you talking about?" Lee asked. "There seem to be a lot of them tonight."

"Reggie first. What a shitty thing to do to your girlfriend."

"Right? I was, and still am, totally shocked by it all." Stuart was numb with shock at this point.

"Then Sergei… What the hell? I thought better of him."

"As I told Stuart, Sergei didn't mean it that way. He is really gutted by all of it. He's the one who called and asked me to make sure Stuart had a ride home when he was done."

"Still…"

"Yeah," Stuart agreed, "still." The next part he almost whispered. "I understand where he is coming from, but I wanted to be a priority, you know?"

Lee replied first. "You *are* a priority. He's very serious about you. He loves you."

"I know that intellectually, but my heart doesn't believe it yet, especially after tonight."

"Don't do anything rash," Paul added. "From what you've said, he's new to this relationship business too. Not everything is always going to be perfect."

"Like you can talk," Stuart scoffed. "You and Chloe have had smooth sailing from the beginning."

"Uh, I hate to burst your bubble, but no, we haven't. Chloe and I actually split for about three months five years ago."

"What? Why didn't you tell me?"

"I didn't want you to know back then. Chloe was working all the time and when she was home, she wasn't really paying attention or listening to me. I thought she was having an affair."

"Chloe wouldn't."

"She didn't, but I thought she did, so I pulled away. It turns out that one of the partners at the firm she was working at was sexually harassing her and she didn't know how to deal with it. She didn't want to upset me by telling me about it. She reported him, but they didn't do anything about it and the partners were making her life hell. She was so wrapped up in her own head that it took her two weeks to realize that I had moved out. By then, I was pissed and totally convinced I was right."

"Oh shit. What happened?"

"She came to my work since I wasn't answering her calls, marched into my office and basically fell apart. It was the first, and hopefully last, time I ever see that happen. We went to counseling—which I highly recommend, by the way—she quit working for that firm and found another job at a place that treats her right." Paul chuckled. "She also makes a point of making sure she kicks her former company's ass whenever she has a case against them."

"And you didn't think to tell me about any of this?"

"I didn't want you to think badly of her—or me. Neither one of us handled the situation correctly, but we learned from it and came out stronger as a couple for it."

"So, you're saying… What *are* you saying? I shouldn't be mad at Sergei?"

"No," Paul and Lee said together before Paul continued. "You have every right to be angry, but it's a shitty situation all around. You and Sergei *are* good together. You have been happier than I've ever seen you these last few months. Don't throw it away because your feelings got hurt. I know your family threw you away, for all intents and purposes, but I truly don't think that was Sergei's intention."

"Oh, it definitely wasn't his intention," Lee said. "He's a basket case right now. He came knocking on my door an hour or so ago. He left his family at the hospital where Natasha is being evaluated. His mother told him he wasn't helping and kicked him out."

Stuart chuckled. "Yeah, I can totally see that."

They pulled into Stuart's driveway and Lee put the car in Park. "Do you want me to come in with you?"

"Nah. I need to eat then shower. I feel absolutely disgusting and I need to process. I don't think I'd be very good company right now. I'll let you go too, Paul. It's late. Get some sleep."

"Okay, but if you need to talk, no matter the time, give me a call. Promise me."

"I promise."

"Good night." Paul hung up the phone and Stuart turned his head to look at Lee. "I really appreciate you coming to get me tonight."

"What are friends for?"

Stuart shrugged, "I've only really ever had Paul. I'm not the most social person in the world, in case you haven't noticed."

"It's okay. I'm not either, but I'm really glad to have you as my friend."

"Me too," he managed to choke out after a moment. "Now"—Stuart reached out and patted Lee on the shoulder—"let me get my sorry self inside so you can go home and climb into bed with your fiancé."

"Stuart," Lee called out as Stuart went to get out of the car, making him pause, "you can call me anytime too. I hope you know that."

Stuart nodded sharply before climbing out of the car and making his way into his house. The next however-long until he could talk to Sergei again was going to be difficult. He'd been working hard to get ahead of his workload at Sergei's request so they could spend the week before Christmas together before the planned trip down to visit Paul and Chloe between Christmas and New Year's. Sergei was supposed to go with him, but who knew if it was going to happen now.

After he wolfed down a sandwich, Stuart plodded upstairs to the master bathroom. The darkened doorway leading into the guest bathroom caught his attention as he walked by. Maybe it was time to start on those last few renovations the house needed. If things worked out with Sergei, he'd be in a good position to sell the house, and if things didn't work out with Sergei, the work would be done.

Decision made, Stuart continued to the master bathroom, where he stripped off and stepped under the hot spray. He was very happy to get the stench of the police station off him. It was probably more of his flop sweat from all the emotions he'd had rolling through him over the last couple hours, but he was going to blame the police station.

He made the conscious decision to stop thinking about it and focused instead on making a list of what he would need for the bathroom and guest room projects. Maybe Lee would want to help. The first thing he needed was a dumpster…

* * * *

Stuart was covered in dust as he ripped out the last of the drywall from the guest bedroom a week later. When he was trying to prep the walls, he had discovered that the previous occupant had actually carved into the drywall in addition to painting it black. There were way too many holes and gouges to repair, so replacement it would be.

His phone rang just as he heaved the final piece into the dumpster that was currently occupying his driveway. The guest bathroom had already been gutted and drywalled and was ready for the plumber he had hired to come the next day to install the new tub, toilet and sink. Once they were in, he could lay the tiles he had purchased for the project. Looking at the display on his phone, Stuart was surprised to see the number for Everyone's Mechanic pop up.

"Hello."

"Hey, Stuart." Stuart was surprised to hear Nikolai's voice on the line.

"Are we supposed to be talking?"

"I'm calling on official garage business. Lee and Kirk are here too."

"What official garage business could we possibly have?" Stuart asked, honestly puzzled. "I don't have any vehicles due for any maintenance."

"I don't know how to tell you this, so I'm going to just say it straight out."

A surge of panic went through Stuart. "You're scaring me, Nikolai. Is everyone okay? Is Sergei okay?"

"Yes," Nikolai was quick to respond. "Everyone is fine. Someone called the shop, though, and went on a rant about how *'Did we know the person who did our website was gay? He's being investigated for inappropriate touching of a male significantly younger than him. Did we really want to do business with a faggot?'* Then they hung up."

"Stuart," Lee continued, "Saul and Eric said they got the phone call too. It seems someone is going through and contacting all the people who have left reviews and such of your business and telling them you're gay and under investigation."

"Well, the gay thing shouldn't be a surprise to anyone. I've never made a secret of it. I mean, I have a pride flag on my website. I would hope most either wouldn't believe it or would call me about the other allegation. I'm not too worried about it."

"Stuart—" Kirk interrupted then paused.

"Yeah?" Stuart was really confused now.

"It was Natasha," Nikolai blurted out.

"*What?*" Stuart was completely shocked. "Why would she do that?"

"I'm guessing in an attempt to get back at you," Kirk answered. "She's going to be really pissed, though, when she finds out she's losing her internship with Saul and Eric now."

"They don't have to do that—" Stuart started, but he was interrupted by a pissed-off Lee.

"Yes, they do. You're our friend and friends stick together."

Another call beeped in and Stuart glanced at his phone to see his mother's church's number flash up on the screen. Stuart sighed. "I've got to go guys. I think the favor I did for my mother's church is about to come back to bite me in the ass."

"Okay," Lee replied. "We'll all be there in a few minutes. Call Officer Parker and have him come over so we can all make our statements and see if there's a way to get her to stop before she makes any more trouble."

"Yeah. Okay. See you in a few." Stuart clicked over to the other call right before it went to voicemail. "Stuart Woods speaking."

"Mr. Woods, this is Pastor Tucker calling. You've been working on our website. I was calling to tell you that your services will no longer be required."

"I'm guessing you received a phone call regarding my gay status. Is that why you suddenly don't need me to continue? My donated services aren't good enough, now that you know I'm gay?"

Obviously sensing danger, the pastor backtracked quickly. "We did receive a phone call, yes, but that's not why we're cancelling. We have decided that you're not taking the website in the direction we want it to go."

"I see. Well, it's not a problem. I don't want to work with anyone who doesn't share or believe in my vision, especially if you are going to believe anonymous phone calls without even hearing my side of the story. Judge not lest ye be judged, eh, pastor? Have a nice day, Pastor Tucker."

Stuart hung up the phone then made his way back inside. He was seething. He couldn't believe the mess Natasha had created. As he closed the door behind him, his phone started to ring again, this time with his mother's ringtone. Stuart banged his head against the back of the door three times before biting the bullet and answering the phone.

"Hello, Mother. How are you?"

"Don't you 'hello, Mother' me. How could you embarrass me this way?"

"You knew I was gay, Mother. I came out to you a long time ago."

"Well yes, but allegations of inappropriate touching? How could you?"

"The fact that you would believe that without even bothering to ask me tells me how you really feel about me. It's not true, but since you haven't cared about my side or feelings about anything in a long time, I doubt it will matter. Don't plan on me for Christmas. I'll spend it with my true family. Goodbye, Mother. Don't bother calling me again."

Stuart hung up the phone and pulled in gulping breaths of air as his mother's ringtone sounded again. He declined the call and pushed the buttons necessary to block her number before turning and pressing his back against the door, sliding down until he was sitting on the floor. He set his phone on the hardwood next to him before banging the back of his head lightly against the door in a futile attempt to get his thoughts to stop spinning. When spots appeared in front of his eyes, he realized he was hyperventilating and focused on pulling air in and out of his lungs for a few moments.

Once he had himself under control — or mostly, at any rate — Stuart picked his phone back up and found the contact information for Officer Parker. He was glad when the officer picked up after only a couple rings.

"Officer Parker."

"Hello. It's Stuart Woods. Do you have time to come over to my house in the next hour or so? It seems that all the people I've done business with are getting ugly phone calls about me."

"Really? That's interesting. Any idea from who?"

"Yeah. They say it's Natasha. Some of the people who have received calls are on their way over here. They want to give statements and see what we can do to get her to stop."

"I was hoping she wasn't going to do anything stupid. Obviously, it was a wasted hope. Give me forty-five minutes to an hour. I'll bring my partner with me. Hopefully, we won't have to take up too much of your time."

"I appreciate it."

"See you soon."

Chapter Sixteen

Sergei paced anxiously in his parents' living room. Officer Parker was on his way over to talk to all of them. Sergei really hoped it was to say the investigation was over and he could talk to Stuart again. He *missed* him. He felt like he had a permanent hole in his chest. It had been a very long couple of weeks. It was two days before Christmas and he really wanted to spend Christmas with his boyfriend — *if* he forgave him.

The doorbell finally rang, announcing Officer Parker's arrival. Sean stood and went to answer the door. Sergei took a deep, calming breath when Officer Parker appeared and strode forward to greet the man and shake his hand.

"Officer, thank you for coming to speak to us. Please tell me the investigation is over and I can talk to Stuart again," Sergei began.

"I'm sorry to bother all of you so close to Christmas. That part of the investigation is over, but there is more I need to discuss with you before you can talk to Stuart."

"More?"

"Yep, and I'm afraid you aren't going to like it."

"Officer Parker," Daria greeted him. "Would you like to take a seat? Can I get you anything to drink first? Coffee? Tea?"

"Nothing for me, ma'am, but thank you for asking."

Daria and Sean sat on either side of Natasha on the couch, while Officer Parker took one of the wingback chairs and Sergei took the other.

After a tense few moments where Sergei tried and failed to read Officer Parker's expression, the man pulled a small notebook out of the breast pocket of his suit coat and glanced at it for a moment before he began to speak.

"As you know, Reginald Worthington was arrested two weeks ago for purchasing a controlled substance from one Jacob Jones. We'd been after him for a while for distributing, mainly pharmaceuticals to the college crowds in Raleigh, but we were never able to catch him in the act."

A disgruntled huff from Natasha had Sergei shooting her a stern look while Daria told her to stop and let the man speak. Officer Parker ignored her and continued to read from his notes.

"Mr. Worthington has accepted a plea deal from the district attorney's office and has admitted to putting liquid Ritalin in Natasha's tea. He says he did it without Natasha knowing, in an attempt to get her to lose weight, as one of the drug's side effects is weight loss. He further admitted he gave her other drugs, mostly over the counter but some prescription, to help her sleep or make her pliable."

"You lie. He wouldn't do that." Natasha crossed her arms over her chest and glared at Officer Parker.

"He did do that, Ms. Hamilton. He admitted to it in writing. Mr. Jones also accepted a plea bargain, so there will be no need for Mr. Woods to testify as to what he witnessed."

Sergei sat forward eagerly. "That means I can talk to Stuart now. Right?" Sergei made a move to stand up, but Officer Parker waved him back into his seat.

"That will depend on how you react to the rest of what I am getting ready to tell you."

"What else is there?" Sergei furrowed his brow in concern.

"It seems your sister didn't like the fact that Mr. Woods was going to testify against her boyfriend, so she's gone out of her way to make his life as difficult as possible."

"What do you mean?" Daria asked while turning to stare at Natasha. "What have you done?"

"Do you want to be the one to tell them, young lady?" At Natasha's stubborn silence, Officer Parker continued. "Why don't we listen to the recording we got off the phones at V&H Sports. Shall we?"

A look of fear crossed over Natasha's face before it was quickly hidden behind a mask of disdain. Officer Parker hit Play on his phone and Eric's voice rang out.

"Eric Hallahan."

Natasha's voice was next. *"You don't know me, but I'm calling to let you know that the man who created and manages your website is accused of inappropriate touching of someone much younger than him. Stuart Woods is a disgusting homosexual, and you would do well to stop using his services before he drags you down with him."*

They all stared at Natasha in horror. Sergei was completely blindsided by the fact that Natasha would do such a thing.

"You can't prove it was me."

"You used your own cell phone and didn't hide the number. We have obtained your phone records and have a list of all the businesses you called. After contacting them ourselves in the course of our investigation, we have found that you gave them the same or very similar messages to what was said to Mr. Hallahan. We *can* prove it was you."

"Natasha Rose Hamilton! How could you?" Daria's voice trembled with emotion as she spoke. Sergei was torn between wanting to go and comfort his mother and not wanting to get too close to Natasha for fear of what he would do to her.

Officer Parker waited for the noise to die down before he cleared his throat to get their attention. "I'm afraid I'm not done." He reached into his breast pocket and retrieved a couple of folded letters. "I have in my hand official documents for you, Ms. Hamilton. First, this is a cease and desist letter from Mr. Woods' lawyer, documented and approved by the courts. He has stated that he will not press charges as long as you receive counseling and treatment for your drug use." He held the letter out to Natasha and waited until she snatched it out of his hand. "Second, I have a letter from V&H, rescinding their offer of internship for the spring semester. As both owners are, one" — Officer Parker held up one finger — "also gay and in committed relationships, and two" — he added a second finger to the count — "great friends with Mr. Woods, they have no desire to associate with you."

"They can't do that," Natasha gasped. "I need the internship to graduate. Sergei, you have to tell them that they can't do that."

Sergei slowly shook his head. "No. I don't think so. You've gone way too far. Do you not get that I *love* Stuart? He's my boyfriend. I hope to one day marry him, and you, in all your pettiness, set out to ruin his business. I just hope you haven't ruined any and all chances for me with him."

"But, Sergei," Natasha shouted, "he got Reggie arrested."

"He was drugging you, Natasha," Sergei shouted back. "What part of him drugging you don't you get? From what Officer Parker just told us, he was drugging you to get you to lose weight and he was giving you other drugs to help counteract the first drug so you would sleep. Stuart is not now, nor has he ever been, the bad guy here."

Natasha went to stand up, but her father snagged her by the arm and forced her to sit back down, then spoke through gritted teeth. "I don't think Officer Parker is done, as he still has one more letter in his hand. You will sit here, and you will listen to everything he has to say."

"But, Daddy," Natasha whined, "they're trying to ruin my life."

"No," Daria cut in sharply, "this disaster is all on you."

Officer Parker waited for Natasha to sit back again with her arms crossed and a defiant look on her face before he spoke again.

"This last document is from your university. As Mr. Worthington's case has come to their attention, they have also been keeping a close eye on you. Mr. Worthington has already spoken to the review committee. He will no longer be a student at the university."

Natasha jumped to her feet. "But he only has one semester left. They can't do that!"

"They can and they did. Now, as I was saying, this final document is from your university. They have learned of your phone calls and conducted an investigation into your recent behaviors. My understanding is that you were drunk and got into a fist fight with another girl last month for daring to look at your boyfriend for too long, meaning that you were already on thin ice with them. Let me just say that they are not any happier with your more recent behavior. As they hope it is simply a matter of getting the drugs and alcohol out of your system, they have decided that you will be suspended for one semester to allow you to get help. It is strongly recommended that you enter a drug and alcohol treatment plan."

"What?" Natasha's pitch rose to ear-shattering levels, making Sergei flinch. "They can't do that!"

"You keep saying that," the officer responded implacably, "but they *can*—and they *did*. Mr. and Mrs. Hamilton, I am very sorry to be the bearer of such bad news."

"It is not of your doing, Officer Parker," Sean said wearily.

"Is Stuart okay? Has he lost a lot of business?"

"This is what you're worried about, Sergei? My life is *ruined*, and you're worried about your *boyfriend*?" Natasha could not have put any more condescension in her tone when she said the word 'boyfriend' if she'd tried.

Sergei stood up. "Yes, and now I have to go talk to my *boyfriend* and beg his forgiveness." Sergei took a step toward the door, only to be stopped by Officer Parker.

"He's not home. He went to visit some friends in Florida. He didn't want to spend Christmas alone."

"What do you mean? I thought he was spending Christmas with his mom?"

"Uh, no. One of the places your sister called was his mom's church. Her church fired him without asking to hear his side. They were, however, the only business who fired him. Everyone else signed complaints against your sister, but Mr. Woods' mother called and yelled at him because she was embarrassed and horrified that he would do such a thing."

Sergei shot his sister a dirty look when she snickered. She must have finally gotten how pissed he was at her, because she flinched back into the couch and dropped her gaze to her lap. Turning his attention back to the officer, he waited for him to continue.

"The only reason I know he left town is because he called and asked if it was okay for him to do so. He left yesterday."

"I see." Sergei put one hand on the wall and hung his head as he thought. Making a decision, he looked up and met his mother's gaze. "Mom, I'm sorry. I won't be here for Christmas. I need to find Stuart and beg his forgiveness for this mess."

Tears appeared in his mom's eyes. "While it will be difficult not having you here for Christmas, we have a mess to clean up here. I believe some research into drug rehab is on the agenda. You tell Stuart that Sean and I are sorry. This is not how we raised Natasha to behave."

"Mom!"

His mother barely spared Natasha a glance at her interruption before she addressed Sergei again. "Go."

Sergei strode forward and gave his mother a quick hug and kiss on the cheek, before turning and hugging Sean when he stood up. He then shook Officer Parker's hand. "Thank you for the information. I don't suppose you have Paul's address in Florida, do you?"

"I do, but I can't give it to you."

Sergei sighed. "That's what I thought. On to Plan B." Pulling out his phone as he headed out of the door, Sergei pulled up the contact for Everyone's Mechanic. He hoped someone there had the information he needed. Nikolai answered the phone after two rings.

"Everyone's Mechanic."

"Hey, Nik. It's Sergei. Is Lee still at the garage today? I need to talk to him." Sergei figured that if anyone knew where Stuart was, it would be Lee. The two of them were tight. He also knew he had some begging to do before Lee would probably tell him anything.

"Yeah. He's still here."

"Okay. Don't let him leave. I'm on my way."

In between calls to his pilot and to his assistant Brandon, Sergei rehearsed what he was going to say to Lee on the drive over to the garage. He pulled into their parking lot, still not having decided what the best approach would be. He walked through the front door to see Nikolai sitting at the desk.

"Kirk said for you to go on through to his office when you got here. They're all waiting for you there."

"All?"

"Yeah. Saul, Eric, Lee and Kirk are all in there."

"Oh." Sergei squared his shoulders and made to walk to the office. It was probably best this way. *Face them all at once.*

He heard Nikolai giggle and he turned to look at him, raising an eyebrow in question.

"Stop looking like you're heading to the gallows. They're your friends too, ya know."

"They were Stuart's friends first, especially Lee."

"You love Stuart more than anything, though. Yeah, you have some making up to do, but it was a weird series of events. They know that," Nikolai said with a wave in the direction of the office.

"Yeah." Sergei turned again, made his way to where everyone was waiting and knocked. At the called 'come in', he entered to find all four of the men staring at him.

"Have a seat," Lee said, indicating an empty chair next to Saul. "We have to leave in like half an hour to get to the airport for our flight to Florida. We promised Saul's mom we would be there for Christmas."

"Well, I'm going to be on my way to Florida shortly too. I need to figure out where exactly in Florida I'm going first, though. Do any of you have Paul's address in Orlando?"

"Have you tried calling Stuart and asking for it?" Kirk asked.

Sergei flushed. "No. I don't want to risk him not answering the phone. I need to see him and be with him for Christmas." *Hold him*, but they didn't need to hear that.

"What about your family?" Saul asked.

"My mother and Sean are currently researching drug rehab places for my sister. My sister is pissed that the world doesn't, in fact, revolve around her. I'm so mad at her right now that it's best that I'm not around her. I can't believe she did that to Stuart. For the rest of it, she was really the victim. The mood swings are understandable once you know about the drugs, but what she did to Stuart and calling all those places was vicious."

"She needed a scapegoat for everything," Lee interjected quietly.

"Then she should have blamed the person actually responsible, not the man I love. It's killed me having to stay away from him, so please. I don't want to be away from him any longer. Where is he?" Sergei was only slightly embarrassed by the pleading tone in his voice.

"It wasn't any easier on him. He doesn't know where he fits in your life. You are a very busy and important man." Lee held up his hand to stop Sergei from speaking. "He knows you love him, but he doesn't trust that you'll keep him. This" — Lee waved his hand in a circle in the air, obviously struggling to find the right word before finally settling on — "debacle... This debacle didn't help in any way, shape or form."

"I know. My traveling all the time didn't help either. I'm working on making some changes in my company structure so I won't have to travel so much, and I'm hopeful Stuart will consider traveling with me when I do have to go somewhere, but these are all things I need to discuss with Stuart. I don't want to have Christmas without him. *Please*. Does one of you have the address?"

Lee and Kirk shared a long look before Lee gave Kirk a nod and Kirk held out a sheet of paper with an address on it.

Kirk didn't let go of the paper right away when Sergei reached for it, making eye contact with him. "We're trusting you to make this right. He's had quite enough bad in his life."

"I will do my best."

"Make sure you do." With a nod, Kirk let go and Sergei looked at the address before pulling out his phone and dialing the number for his pilot.

"Rob, is your family okay to fly to Orlando a few days earlier than planned?"

"Yep. The wife has us all packed up. Thanks for taking care of extending our hotel and all that."

"No problem. I had Brandon handle it. Hey, hang on a minute." Turning to Lee and Saul, he asked, "where are you guys flying to? If it's Orlando, you can join me on my plane instead of flying commercial, if you're interested."

"My folks are about an hour north of Orlando. That's where we were flying into. We have a rental car from there."

"So? Commercial or with me? Full disclosure, my pilot's family will also be on the plane and he has a five- and a seven-year-old on their way to Disney for the first time."

Sergei watched a smile cross Lee's face. "Oh, definitely with you. Our bags are in the car. Kirk was going to run us to the airport so we didn't have to pay a fortune for parking for the week. Did you want to go pack a bag and we can swing by and pick you up on the way to the airport?"

"That would actually be great." Pulling the phone from his chest, Sergei asked Rob to add two more passengers to the flight manifest, hanging up after Rob assured him it would be done.

"Okay. Give me half an hour to pack and I'll be ready to go."

"Great. See you in a few then."

* * * *

By the time Sergei had made it on to the plane, he was hanging on to his nerves by a thread. He couldn't remember a time when he had been so scared. *What if Stuart refuses to speak to me? What if he doesn't want anything to do with me and my family ever again? What if —* His spiraling thoughts were interrupted by Lee.

"You need to breathe."

"What?"

"You are spinning there, dude. It's written all over your face. He loves you. Yes, you have some groveling to do, but he loves you."

"I hope it's enough."

Lee scoffed. "Like you would ever let him go. I've never known you to give up on anything."

Sergei felt a surge of confidence at Lee's words. "You're right. I'm not letting him go. He's going to have to accept it. We're meant to be together."

"That's the spirit," Saul cheered from his seat on the other side of Lee.

Sergei settled back in his seat and closed his eyes for a few moments. Luckily, it wasn't a long flight from Raleigh to Orlando, so he didn't have too much time to fret. The kids had been surprisingly well-behaved — or maybe not so surprisingly. He'd traveled with Rob's family before. Rob's wife was exceptionally well organized. She said it mainly came from first being a military brat then a military spouse while Rob had been in the Air Force.

After they collected their luggage and exited the plane, the three distinct groups headed to the car rental counter. With three sets of keys procured, they made their way to the reserved vehicles. After saying his goodbyes to everyone, Sergei climbed into the luxury car he had rented and put Paul's address into his phone to let the voice navigator direct him.

Arriving at a well-maintained house not far from Disney, Sergei climbed out of the car. He wasn't quite confident enough to bring his luggage in with him. He would have to wait to see what happened. Stepping up on the porch, he was getting ready to ring the doorbell when the door was jerked open. He found himself confronted by a red-headed woman who had to be close to six feet tall and she was not happy to see him.

"Do not touch that doorbell if you wish to live."

"Why would ringing the doorbell result in a death sentence?"

A look of surprise crossed her face. "You're Sergei."

"Yes. How did you know?"

"The accent and the bespoke suit, genius. What are you doing here?"

"I've come to spend Christmas with my boyfriend."

"Does he know you are coming?"

"No. I wished it to be a surprise."

A calculating look crossed her face next. "You didn't want him to tell you 'no' is more like it."

Sergei shrugged. "The possibility did perhaps play into my decision. Yes. I am guessing you are Chloe?"

"Yes." When she didn't say anything else, he continued. "Is Stuart here?"

"Yes, but he is currently napping with my children. He is the only one who can get my son to sleep and they have only been sleeping for about a half hour. If you wake him, there will be hell to pay." Chloe crossed her arms over chest and raised her chin at him militantly.

"Ah, now the no-doorbell thing makes sense. May I at least see Stuart? I promise I will not wake anyone. I just need to see that he is okay."

"Physically he's fine." Chloe narrowed her gaze at Sergei. "Emotionally is another story. If you're here to hurt him more…" She let the threat trail off.

"Most people are scared of me, you know," Sergei huffed out.

"Ha. Most people don't know you through the eyes of a man totally in love with you. I am giving you a chance to make it right. Don't screw this up again."

As they had been talking, she had been leading him through the house and to an open sliding glass door looking out onto the screened-in lanai. Sergei could see Stuart lying in a hammock with a dark-haired child of maybe six months on his chest and a little redheaded girl sleeping against his shoulder. Stuart had one arm supporting the little boy and the other arm wrapped around the little girl, keeping them both secure. His heart absolutely melted at the sight. He *wanted* that.

"Oh."

Chloe's whisper startled him. He'd forgotten she was there for a moment as he drank in the sight of his boyfriend.

"What?" Sergei tore his gaze away from the vision in front of him with difficulty.

"You want that." Chloe waved a hand in the direction of Stuart and the sleeping children. "Stuart and the children and the whole nine yards. You really do love him."

"I do." Sergei nodded to show his sincerity. "I love him and want it all with him."

She assessed him for another long moment before she nodded back. "You'll do. Come on. Stuart says you're a good cook. Come help me with dinner."

Chapter Seventeen

"Uncle Tu-Tu."

Stuart woke up to the sound of his honorary niece calling his name — or her version of it anyway. She had heard her dad call him Stu-Stu one day and thought it was funny. Since she couldn't say her Ss well yet, he'd become Uncle Tu-Tu. Paul, of course, found it hysterical.

"Yeah, Katie, what do you need?" Stuart asked around a yawn, trying to keep his voice low so they wouldn't wake Jack.

"I have to go potty."

"Okay. Go ahead. Your mommy is inside."

"Okie dokie."

Stuart put down a foot to steady the hammock as Katie climbed out and went running off. He closed his eyes again but reopened them when he thought he heard Sergei's accented voice introducing himself to Katie. His head turned in the direction of the open door. Surely he hadn't heard Sergei. He must be hearing things. *Man, I'm losing it.* He covered his mouth as another yawn forced its way out. Looking at the watch on his wrist, he saw that he and the kids had been asleep for a little over two hours. Sensing a presence at the door, he looked up to find Chloe standing there. At the same time, Jack started to do his cute little wiggle, which indicated he was trying to wake up too.

"What's up?" Stuart called.

"Hand me Jack. Dinner will be ready shortly, but you have a visitor."

"I really did hear Sergei a few minutes ago then?"

"Yep. Your niece is currently in the kitchen working her charms on him, trying to get him to sneak her a cookie." Chloe stepped forward as she spoke and took her son from Stuart's chest, allowing Stuart to swing his legs around then climb out of the hammock while she disappeared back into the house.

He stood there for a moment and ran his hand through his hair, attempting to wake up a bit more before he followed her, but he paused when he saw Sergei standing in the doorway.

He shoved his hands into his pockets, not really knowing what to say. "Hi." Well, that might not have been intelligent, but it was all he had.

"Hi." Seeing Sergei just as nervous as he was settled something in him.

"What are you doing here?"

"Where else would I be? It's Christmas. I should be with my boyfriend."

"Yeah? Am I still your boyfriend?"

"Until you are my fiancé then husband, yeah."

"You sound so certain."

"Well, since I'm not ever letting you go…"

"What about your family?"

"First, I want to apologize for my sister trying to ruin your business. She had no right to do such a thing." Stuart couldn't doubt his sincerity from the look on his face.

"That's not for you to apologize for."

"I know, but I will anyway. I would like to think she will apologize herself once all the drugs are out of her system."

"Drugs, as in multiple?"

"Yeah. It turns out her boyfriend had been giving her quite a cocktail of different things, mostly over-the-counter stuff. My parents are forcing her to enter rehab after her latest stunt, but as you and others have told me many times, my sister is not my responsibility. She's an adult now and she needs to live her own life, make her own decisions and face the consequences for them." Sergei took another step toward Stuart as he searched Sergei's face for any signs of regret.

"Are you okay with that?" Stuart asked and was aware how important Sergei's answer would be.

Sergei was now close enough that he could reach out and take hold of Stuart's hand. "Yes. I find that I'm going to be too busy making sure my boyfriend knows he is the most important person in my life."

"Next to your mother, of course," Stuart said with a chuckle.

Sergei simply raised an eyebrow at Stuart.

"What? You can't mean... You protected your sister against me." Stuart remembered the pain and anger of that moment and pulled his hand from Sergei's.

"I knew you would regret it if you were forced to protect yourself against her. I was protecting you, not her. She was out of control."

"Agreed, but…" Stuart let his words trail off, as he had no idea what he wanted to say. His mind was a whirlwind of different thoughts and emotions.

"I love you, Stuart. I have had a hole where my heart should be during these weeks when we could not be in contact with one another."

"They wanted to make sure you wouldn't talk me out of testifying. They've been trying to catch that guy for a long time."

"I know this logically. Emotionally, I've been a mess. It was not a feeling that I or the people around me have enjoyed, to be honest. I need you with me. You are my best friend as well as my lover. I've missed you."

"I've missed you too," Stuart allowed quietly. "But I don't know if I could survive it if we became even more serious and you decided to walk away."

Sergei reached out, grabbed Stuart by the arms and pulled him into his embrace. "There is no one more serious for me. I told you. You are only my boyfriend until we get married and we will be married forever. I thought my heart was going to explode out of my chest when I saw you sleeping out here with Paul's children. I want the whole thing with you — the house, the family."

"You do?"

"Yes." Sergei pressed a kiss to Stuart's lips. "I want it all, but only with you. We will make beautiful children one day."

Stuart felt a spurt of amusement go through him "You do realize you can't actually knock me up, right?"

"Ha, ha. You need to work on your jokes, Tu-Tu."

"Ugh. Never me call me that again."

Sergei laughed the robust, uninhibited laugh that Stuart so rarely heard. All his guards were down, allowing Stuart to see the most private parts of him. In that moment, he realized Sergei truly was all in. The question was, was he brave enough to be the same?

Sergei must have seen the doubt on his face or in his eyes, something, because he tightened his arms around Stuart. "Accept it. I'm not letting you go. We need to figure out how to make this work so that we're both happy. I love you."

Sergei then pressed his lips to Stuart's, demanding his tongue's entrance. A yell interrupted their moment, startling them apart.

"Mommy! Uncle Sir is kissing Uncle Tu-Tu!"

Chloe's voice, tinged with amusement, came from inside. "Well, tell them dinner's ready. They'll have to wait until later for kissing."

"Uncle Tu-Tu, Mommy said —"

"We heard her, Katie. We're coming." Stuart gave Sergei a peck on the lips. "Distracting me with kisses doesn't mean everything is solved, but we'll talk later okay?"

"We will definitely be talking and kissing later, *kotik*."

"Talking first, babe."

"Agreed...unless you simply can't hold yourself back any longer."

Stuart couldn't help laughing at this playful side of Sergei as he turned to make his way into the house. "Down, babe. Your ego is showing."

"Is that what we're calling it now?" Paul's question, from where he was sitting at the table drinking a beer, made him jump. Stuart hadn't seen him sitting there.

"Hey, Paul. When did you get back?"

"About a half hour ago. I've been getting to know your boyfriend here." Paul pointed the mouth of his beer bottle in Sergei's direction. "He's passed the Chloe test, but he's still on probation with me. Just remember that I know people."

Stuart snorted. "You don't know anybody."

Paul shot him a disgusted look. "I could. You don't know everyone I know."

"You work with a mouse."

"Boys, that's enough," Chloe cut in. "Paul, be nice. Sergei knows he has some making up to do. Right, Sergei?"

"Yes, ma'am. I will not let you down."

Paul sighed. "Why does she get respect and I get laughed at?"

Stuart pressed his lips together to keep the snicker in. "Um, you have met your wife, right?"

"Yeah. Yeah. Whatever. I'm starving. Let's eat."

Stuart snuck looks at Sergei throughout dinner, most of the time finding Sergei looking at him too. Katie had obviously decided he was amazing and had insisted Sergei sit next to her and be the one to help her with anything she needed for dinner. She was currently telling Sergei all about her best friend Alicia, who had gotten in trouble at preschool that day for punching a boy in the nose.

"Why would she punch him in the nose?" It was fun to see Sergei hanging on Katie's every word. She obviously had him wrapped around her little finger already.

"He said Spider-Man was better than Batman."

"And? Can't you each have your favorites?"

"Well, yeah, but not when he said she was just a stupid girl and she didn't know what she was talking about."

"What?" Chloe interrupted. "You didn't tell me that part."

"You didn't ask," Katie said with three-, almost four-year-old logic.

"Did she tell the teacher that part?"

"No-o-o." Katie dragged out the word to three syllables. "The teacher didn't ask either. She asked if Alicia punched him and she said yes."

"Excuse me a moment," Chloe said, standing up from the table. "I'd better call Alicia's parents and make sure they know everything. Her mom was pretty upset that she had punched somebody." She leveled a stern look at Katie. "You shouldn't punch people for saying mean things to you either, though. You should tell the teacher."

"But that's tattling."

"Not when someone is being mean."

"Adam is always mean, though. Maybe he won't be so mean now that he knows Alicia can kick his butt."

Chloe opened her mouth then closed it again without anything coming out. She shook her head as she turned and went to grab her phone. "We will discuss it later."

Stuart had to work hard not to laugh and he looked up and saw Sergei was struggling as well. He didn't dare look at Paul. Paul was his kryptonite when it came to inappropriate laughter.

Stuart cleared his throat. "What have you been up to the last couple weeks, Sergei?"

"I've been working to try to figure out what I can do so I don't have to travel as much."

"Why? You love your job," Stuart said.

"I love my boyfriend more and I want to spend more time with him," Sergei replied matter-of-factly.

"Really? You'd do that for me?"

"For us, yes. I'm hopeful you can travel with me when I do have to go somewhere, otherwise I'm learning to delegate a bit more." Sergei held Stuart's gaze.

Stuart's cheeks hurt because he was smiling so wide, but he couldn't seem to make himself stop. "I can mostly do my work from anywhere, as long as I have Wi-Fi. I would certainly consider traveling with you."

"Yeah?" Sergei's answering smile was just as wide.

"Yeah."

Paul interrupted their moment. "Oh, for goodness sakes. You two are sappy. I'm trying to eat here."

"Like you aren't the same way with Chloe."

"He's worse, actually." Chloe said as she reentered the room. "You didn't see him when I was pregnant. I swear he worried that a paperclip was too heavy for me."

"We aren't talking about me," Paul said indignantly. "We're talking about those two."

"Leave them alone, dear. They're newly reunited. We're lucky to even have them at the dinner table with us."

"Why? Aren't they hungry?" Katie's question reminded them there were little ears present.

Sergei was the first to answer. "Yes, Katie, we are very hungry, and I, for one, am very happy to eat dinner with all of you. It is my pleasure to meet Stuart's family."

"Yep. He's my favoritest uncle."

"I'm your *only* uncle," Stuart grumped at her fondly.

Katie shrugged. "Still my favoritest."

"Eat your dinner, Katie."

"Is everything good with Alicia's parents?" Paul asked Chloe.

"Yeah. They are going to have a talk with the teacher tomorrow about the whole thing. What were you all talking about?"

"Sergei was telling Stuart he is trying to fix things so that he doesn't have to travel so much."

"That's great. I know Stuart will love having you around more."

"It will be nice." Stuart shot another look at Sergei and gave him a smile.

"What have you been up to the last few weeks?" Sergei asked Stuart.

"Well, as you know, I had been working to get ahead so I could take the last couple weeks of the year off. I found myself at loose ends and decided to tackle the guest bedroom and the hall bath."

"You did? I was going to help you with those. Please, tell me you didn't do it all by yourself."

"No. I had a plumber come in and install the new tub, toilet and sink. Lee came over and helped me with some of the rest, but I did do most of it myself. It turned out really great. It's a huge improvement, at any rate."

"I can't wait to see it."

Stuart was surprised to see a hint of sadness in Sergei's eyes. "What?"

"I was looking forward to working on the projects with you."

"Oh. I'm sorry. I needed something to do instead of mope, though."

"I can certainly understand that." Displaying one of his mercurial mood changes, Sergei smiled. "Of course, this means that you'll have more time for me. That is a good thing." With a decisive nod, Sergei turned toward the little boy on his left, who had thrown a green bean at him. "You know, throwing food's not very nice. You are supposed to eat the green beans, not throw them."

Jack grinned at him unrepentantly, obviously not bothered by the chastisement, and he picked up another green bean and threw it at Sergei. This time it landed in his hair.

Stuart couldn't help the laugh that exploded out of him.

"You find this funny?" Sergei asked.

"Yep," Stuart choked out. "The impeccable Sergei with a green bean in his hair. Let me get a picture." Stuart pretended to reach into his pocket for his phone but started laughing harder when Sergei growled at him as he picked the green bean out. "Aw, babe. There is no need to get growly."

"You are *so* not funny, *kotik*."

"What does *kotik* mean?" Katie asked with an adorable scrunch in her nose.

"It means 'kitten' in Russian."

"You call Uncle Tu-Tu 'kitten'?"

"Yep and he calls me 'babe' or 'Rabbit' from Winnie the Pooh."

"I like Tigger. He's my favoritist. He's bouncy." Katie demonstrated by bouncing in her chair.

"Enough. Everyone finish eating. It's getting late and it's bath time for little girls."

"Aw, Mom."

"You heard me. If you two are done, why don't you go get Sergei's luggage out of the car and head to the guest cottage? I know you have a lot to talk about still."

"Yeah…talk." Paul added a suggestive waggle to his eyebrows, which made Stuart snort.

"So subtle and mature, dork, but I'm not going to turn down a chance to get Sergei alone. Are you done eating?"

"Oh yes. Guest cottage?"

"Chloe and Paul had a mini cottage built at the back of their property. It has its own bathroom, but that's about it."

"But it's private," Chloe added, "and if the doors and windows are closed, we won't be able to hear a thing. We made sure it was sound-proofed for any and all guests."

Paul stage-whispered to them, "What she's not saying is that her father snores like a freight train and it's better if he's away from the main house when he visits."

Stuart snickered. "Oh yeah. Remember when we went on that fishing trip?"

Paul nodded emphatically. "It was bad — and what prompted the decision to build the guest cottage. I think he probably scared the bears in the area. I'm pretty sure that's why we didn't catch any fish too."

"Probably so," Stuart agreed. "On that note, I'm taking Sergei to show him my etchings. We will see you all in the morning."

"See your etchings? Really?" Sergei asked, sounding disgusted.

"What? Don't you want to see my etchings?" Stuart asked as innocently as he could.

"Come on," Sergei growled as he snagged his hand and pulled Stuart behind him out of the door to his car so he could grab his bags.

Once they had made it to the guest cottage, Stuart was hit with a sudden case of nerves. He wandered around the space, picking up the little odds and ends that had spread out over the last couple days. He heard Sergei drop his bags next to the door before Sergei suddenly grabbed and spun Stuart into his arms.

"Leave it. Everything is fine. There's no reason to be nervous." Sergei leaned in and took Stuart's mouth in one of his patented heated kisses as soon as he stopped speaking. "I love you. I missed you. I need you. *Gah!* I've turned into a sap." Sergei released Stuart and took a step back.

"What's the matter?"

"I'm terrified that you're going to send me away. Everything has sucked the last couple of weeks without you. I always swore I would never let anyone but family in, but you snuck by and I don't know how to handle this." Sergei pointed between the two of them several times.

"Our relationship?"

"Yes...that."

Stuart couldn't help but smile to see the normally unflappable Sergei Barinov coming undone.

"Do you think it's any easier for me? I don't have great role models like your parents who show that a relationship can be a partnership. My stepfather is in control of everything. It's been great seeing Kirk and Eric and Saul and Lee each have loving partnerships, but I was equal parts scared it would never happen for me and terrified that I would become less if I found someone."

"You could never become less. You have such a strong core and sense of self. It's one of the many things I love about you." Sergei took a deep breath and released it noisily. "How about this... How about we work on being strong together? I've missed you so much, and I'm definitely stronger with you than without you. You make me a better person. Now, come here." Sergei opened his arms then stepped forward to meet Stuart in the middle of the small space and pull him into a strong hug.

"You really believe that?"

"Believe what?"

"That we're stronger together?"

"Don't you?"

Stuart paused to think for a moment. "Yeah. I guess we are. I know I'm much happier with you than without you. Your family doesn't hate me?"

"No. They love you too. My mother told me to tell you they were sorry."

"What? They have nothing to apologize for."

"She will be happy to hear you feel that way. Now, I believe we have better things to do with our time than discuss my family."

"Oh yeah? Are we going to practice the baby-making for our future brood?"

"Yeah," Sergei agreed with a chuckle, "that's it." Sergei grabbed hold of the bottom of Stuart's shirt and pulled it up and over his head then ran his hands down Stuart's chest, tweaking his nipples on the way past before leaning in and kissing him.

Stuart reached between them and started working on the buttons of Sergei's dress shirt—untucking the shirt as he reached the bottom then pushing it off his shoulders, frustrated by the fact that he was wearing a T-shirt underneath the dress shirt. "You are wearing too many damn layers. Get undressed."

Stuart stepped back and worked on removing the rest of his clothing then watched as Sergei finished. They stared at each other for a long moment. The tension in the air ratcheted up with every breath. Stuart trembled because he didn't know what he wanted to do first.

"Get on the bed, Stuart. Let me love you."

With a nod, Stuart turned and made his way to the bed on the other side of the room. Climbing up, he looked over his shoulder when he heard Sergei groan and he found his boyfriend's gaze fixed on his ass. He wiggled it and watched in amazement as Sergei's pupils dilated even more before he strode across the room and tackled him to the bed.

"Please, tell me you have stuff."

"Um, yeah. I put it in the bedside table there." Stuart pointed to the table on the right side of the bed, where he had stashed lube and condoms.

Sergei stared into the drawer for a moment. "You knew I would come for you."

"Hoped. I *hoped* you would, but why would you say that?"

"Because you brought condoms. You are not the type for one-night stands. The fact that you brought condoms shows that a part of you knew I would be here."

Stuart had to swallow hard before he could speak. "Yeah. I hoped."

"Oh, love. I'm here. I will always come for you." Sergei dropped the items on the bed then pushed Stuart over to lie on his back before covering him with his body and kissing him. It started as more of an emotional kiss than a sexual one, but it slowly changed, and they pressed closer and closer until Sergei was completely on top of Stuart, rubbing their bodies together.

Stuart pulled back with a gasp. "Please. I need you in me. *Please*."

Sergei reached for the lube as he rolled to Stuart's side. Slicking his fingers, he pressed first one then two into Stuart, stretching them until he could fit a third finger in. In between, he pressed kisses anywhere he could reach while Stuart stroked his cock until he thought he was going to explode. Stuart groped for the condom and thrust it at Sergei.

"In me. *Now*. I don't want to come until you're in me."

"You are so bossy." Sergei leaned in and took another quick kiss but didn't argue. He took the condom from Stuart and tore open the wrapper, making quick work of rolling it down his member. "This is going to be fast. I'm on the edge here."

"Do it." Stuart grabbed his legs and pulled them back.

Sergei moved into the space and press his cock to Stuart's fluttering hole. He pressed in slowly but steadily, filling the emptiness inside Stuart. It wasn't only the physical. It felt like Sergei was also filling the hole in his soul. Stuart laughed with joy when Sergei was finally all the way inside him.

Sergei pulled back to look at him. "What?"

"I feel good — the best I've felt in weeks — but I know you can make it even better. Move, Barinov."

Sergei put Stuart's legs up on his shoulders and straightened. Stuart's hips lifted off the bed and Sergei grabbed hold of them as he started pressing and retreating until he was pounding into Stuart. Stuart took one of the hands he had knotted in the bedspread to hold himself steady and started to stroke himself in time with Sergei's thrusts.

"Please, *kotik*. You need to come. You feel too good. It's been so long. You have to come first. Stuart!" Sergei's strangled yell of Stuart's name was accompanied by the stuttering of his hips as he emptied into the condom. The feel of Sergei coming inside him sent Stuart over the edge himself and he was coming so hard that he saw stars.

* * * *

Stuart didn't know how long it was before he felt a warm cloth cleaning him. He certainly hadn't felt Sergei pulling out or getting up. "Wow. I've never been fucked so hard that I passed out before." He looked up to see Sergei with a smug look on his face. "Proud of yourself?"

"Immensely. Now move over. I'm exhausted. I have discovered I don't sleep well without you."

Stuart couldn't help laughing at the disgruntled tone of Sergei's voice. "Well, I don't sleep well without you either, so we're even." Stuart yawned loudly as he finished the sentence. Scooting over, he climbed under the covers then held them up for Sergei to slide into bed next to him. Once Sergei was settled, Stuart rolled over and laid his head on Sergei's broad chest, uttering a sigh of contentment when Sergei held him closer. Stuart heard him say something, but he couldn't make it out over the beat of his boyfriend's heart and didn't have the energy to ask him to repeat it. He drifted off to sleep on the thought that he would have find out what it was the next day.

Epilogue

"Valentine's Day. How did it get to be Valentine's Day already?"

Stuart was talking to himself as he drove home — home being Sergei's house. It turned out that what Sergei had asked him when he was falling asleep was if Stuart would move in with him. Stuart had been shocked. He hadn't been sure they were at the cohabitating point yet but he had allowed Sergei to convince him between Christmas and New Year's that it was the right decision. If a lot of that persuasion involved sex, who was Stuart to complain? Stuart grinned to himself as he turned onto their street.

He was surprised to see a catering van outside their house. As far as he knew, they were planning a quiet Valentine's Day dinner in, with just the two of them. After parking his car in the garage, he made his way into the house. "Sergei?"

Stuart heard running footsteps before Sergei appeared in the kitchen, looking frazzled. "What are you doing home already? I thought I had another twenty minutes."

"The meeting finished up faster than I thought it would. What's going on?"

Sergei dropped his head back and stared at the ceiling for a moment. Stuart was surprised to realize that his boyfriend was nervous.

"What's going on, Sergei?" Stuart stepped forward as he asked the question and pulled him into his arms. Sergei dropped his head onto Stuart's shoulder and he heard Sergei mumble something. "What was that?"

Sergei lifted his head and repeated, "I wanted everything to be perfect."

"And I'm sure everything will be. You know I'm not hard to please."

"Okay. Come with me." Sergei stepped back and grabbed Stuart by the hand. Walking into the dining room, Stuart was amazed to find the table set for two, complete with lit candles and covered plates of food. A couple of people in catering uniforms were putting the finishing touches on something, before they turned and greeted the two of them.

"Gentlemen," the taller of the two men said, "your meal is all set. We will get out of your way now. Have a wonderful evening."

"Thank you, gentlemen, I appreciate it. Stay right here," Sergei instructed Stuart as he escorted the men out of the room. Stuart heard the front door open then close then Sergei's footsteps as he returned to stand beside him. "Happy Valentine's Day!" Sergei leaned in and gave Stuart a kiss. He placed a hand at the small of Stuart's back to guide him to the table then pulled out a chair for him to sit in.

Stuart was even more confused by Sergei's behavior when he realized Sergei's hand was shaking as he pulled out his own chair and sat down. "What's going on, love?"

Sergei stared at Stuart for a long moment, obviously looking for something. Stuart tried to show Sergei all the love he held for the man in the hope that it would calm him down. The message must have gotten through, because Sergei visibly calmed before nodding his head as if he had made some sort of decision. Standing back up, Sergei came around the table to Stuart's side. Sergei placed a hand on Stuart's shoulder to keep him sitting.

"No. Stay there. I was going to do this after dinner while we were dancing. There was a whole plan, but I can't wait any longer." Going down to one knee, Sergei pulled a small square box out of his pocket and opened it to show the two titanium bands nestled in the velvet. "I love you. I never want to be without you. Please say you'll marry me."

Stuart tore his gaze away from the rings to look into Sergei's eyes. "Of course I'll marry you. I love you too." Stuart reached out and hauled Sergei into his arms for a hug, followed by a kiss.

"Thank God." Sergei reached into the box, pulled out one of the rings and slipped it onto Stuart's finger, raising Stuart's hand to his lips to bestow a reverent kiss on the ring.

"My turn." Stuart grabbed the second ring out of the box and slid it onto Sergei's ring finger, raising Sergei's hand to place his own kiss. Stuart leaned in and placed a kiss on Sergei's lips before pulling back and looking at him. Stuart pulled Sergei into another hug and quick kiss, then he gestured for Sergei to stand. "Come on.

Let's eat. Everything smells so good. I really appreciate you doing all this for me.

"Yeah. Well, I'm starving. I didn't eat much today."

"You weren't worried I was going to say no, were you?"

"Huh? Oh well," Sergei mumbled something under his breath as he stood to made his way back to his seat.

"You *were* worried." Stuart couldn't help his chuckle at Sergei's discomfiture.

"Maybe a little," Sergei conceded.

"There was no need to be worried. You know I love you."

"Yeah, and you know I love you too." Sergei smiled crookedly at Stuart for a moment. Then he looked away and started uncovering all the dishes on the table.

Stuart was shocked — although thinking about it, he didn't know why — to see all his favorites being revealed. "Wow. You really outdid yourself here. We'll be eating leftovers for a week."

Sergei shot Stuart his normal cocky grin. "And that's not a bad thing."

The two men served themselves and started to eat the wonderful meal. Stuart suddenly remembered he had something to share with Sergei. "Oh, Natasha called me today."

"She did?" Sergei was obviously very surprised by this news and Stuart was warmed by the concern he saw in his eyes. "What did she say?"

"She actually called to apologize. I guess it's something that her therapist suggested she do. She said she was very sorry for the way she acted and she's happy that we found each other. She said everyone else in the family adores me and she knows that she will too in time."

Sergei sat back in his chair. "Wow. That's great."

"Yeah. She really had a rough time of it. Detoxing from all the things her boyfriend was slipping her was not easy, I know."

"I'm grateful you aren't the type to hold a grudge. No one would blame you if you did."

"Eh. Life's too short. Speaking of which, did you say something about dancing?"

"Yep. Come on, *kotik*. Let's dance, then we'll take our dessert upstairs while we seal the deal on this whole engagement."

Stuart laughed as he took the hand Sergei held out to him and allowed him to pull him into the living room, where Sergei had low music playing out of the speakers. Settling into his arms, Stuart was happier than he could ever remember being. "Whose turn is it to lead?"

"How about I start, and you can lead the next one?"

"Hm. That sounds like a perfect plan to me." Stuart leaned forward and gave Sergei a gentle kiss on the lips before he pressed their cheeks together and let Sergei lead him in a slow circle around the room, knowing that he was right where he was supposed to be.

Want to see more like this?
Here's a taster for you to enjoy!

Truth and Beauty
Cassidy Ryan

Excerpt

In the space of half a heartbeat, Alex Jennings went from sound asleep to wide awake, eyes darting around the room, hands clutching at the bed as a sound like the loudest thunder he had ever heard rumbled through the house. The glass light fixture over the bed rattled and the pile of coins he'd stacked on the bedside table the night before tipped over, spilling over the table and onto the hardwood floor.

When the shock of his rude awakening started to subside, and his heart rate had returned to something resembling normal, a scowl pulled Alex's eyebrows together. Pushing the covers aside, he swung his legs over the side of the bed, got to his feet and moved quickly over the cool floor out into the hallway and down the stairs, cursing darkly under his breath.

The rumbling—banging—got louder as he approached his father's office at the back of the house, and just as Alex shoved the door open there was an ear-splitting crash. Dear God, he felt like he had been on a three-day bender. He had to get a place of his own soon. It was fast becoming clear to him that living with one's parents when one was over thirty was nothing less than a shortcut to the mad house.

"Dad?" When there was no response, Alex cursed again and reluctantly moved further into the room. "Dad!"

Seated behind the drum kit, Robert Jennings was grinning like a loon, sweat dampening his thinning, sandy blond hair, arms flailing like he was having some kind of seizure. Robert's body jolted every time one of the sticks in his hands made contact with the drums, and when the cymbals made another discordant, screaming crash, a small grunt of pleasure that was — to Alex at least — quite disturbing, escaped his dad.

Alex moved to stand right in front of the drums, grimacing at the way the floor trembled under his feet and the noise reverberated through him. He could practically feel it bouncing off his bones and liquidising his organs.

"Dad!" Even at the top of his voice, Alex could barely hear himself over the cacophony, but his dad finally opened his eyes and, after taking a moment to focus, his grin became even wider.

"Alex! What do you think? Sounding good, right?" Robert made no move to stop, but actually seemed to pick up the tempo.

Fearing for his long-term hearing, Alex made a slicing motion with his hand across his throat. Robert stopped drumming so suddenly that the silence nearly knocked Alex on to his backside.

"Something I can do for you, son?" Robert's hands were still moving, tapping the drumsticks together almost absently, as if he'd forgotten how to remain still.

"Dad, it's barely eight o'clock in the morning. Do you have to do that right now?" Alex's ears were throbbing like he'd spent a night clubbing.

"I've got to practise." Robert Jennings, sixty-two-year-old former dentist, sounded like a sullen teenager.

Dragging a hand through his hair, Alex stared incredulously at the man who had once been so...sane. "For what, Dad? Are The Who holding auditions?"

"Dude, you're harshing my buzz." Robert spun one of the drumsticks between his fingers in a way that, if Alex hadn't been so dumbfounded, he would probably have found pretty impressive.

As it was, his jaw dropped and he sputtered, sounding like he was being strangled. "Harshing...what? Dude? What the fu..." He managed to cut off the curse before it fully formed, because, even though the man across from him was acting like someone Alex would cross the street to avoid, he was still his dad.

"Don't the neighbours ever complain?" When he was a child growing up on this street, all it had taken for the residents to work up a head of steam was a boisterous game of hide and seek. Alex found it incredible that they weren't threatening his dad with legal action at least for the seismic racket that must be emanating from the house.

Robert shook his head, and, grin returning, executed a drum roll that Alex felt in his teeth.

"These old houses are pretty solid, and, even if they weren't, everyone around here will be on their way to work by now." He was practically glowing with the smug satisfaction of the recently retired.

Alex shook his head and turned towards the door. "Can you just...try not to bring the house down?" He pulled the door closed behind him and got two steps down the hall before the floor started to rumble under his feet again. Knowing that there wasn't a chance in hell that he was going to get any more sleep, Alex headed to the kitchen to make himself some coffee.

As the percolator dripped and gurgled, he went to stand in front of the window and a smile tugged at the corners of his mouth. Out in the back garden his mother was scattering some kind of grain for the chickens pecking at her feet. Chickens. Alex shook his head again. Was it even legal to keep livestock in residential London? The neighbours must think his parents had both gone stark raving bonkers.

Turning away to take a mug from the cupboard, Alex picked up the phone when it rang and tucked it between his ear and shoulder as he poured his coffee.

"Hello?"

"Jennings, you bastard. I know where you are."

Laughter bubbled up in Alex and a wide smile curled his mouth. "Damian! How the hell are you?" He added sugar to his coffee and took the mug over to sit at the table.

"I'm pissed off with you, is how I am. You've been back nearly a month and I had to find out from that arsehole Andy Rowan!" Damian Stanhope didn't sound pissed off — Alex could hear the smile in his best friend's voice.

"Sorry, man, I was going to call you when I got my head on straight. The only reason Andy Rowan knows I'm back is because my mum's friends with his mum." Alex sipped on his coffee, slouching back with a soft sigh when his dad took a break from the drumming. He didn't add that he just hadn't been fit for company, and had been virtually a hermit since stepping over his parents' threshold.

"So, how was Africa?" Damian's voice sounded a little rough, like he'd only recently woken up himself.

Alex caught a glimpse of his mum outside, laughing as she dodged the chickens, and thought about his dad's manic expression as he beat out his dissonant rhythm.

"Sane," he replied, taking another sip of his coffee. Mostly, an inner voice supplied, but Alex slammed the door on it.

"Sane? Okay. I expected life-altering, enlightening, or even just hot, but I suppose sane is good." Alex couldn't help laughing at the confusion in his friend's voice.

He hooked his foot around the leg of another chair and dragged it out so that he could prop his feet up on it. "It's a long story. Suffice it to say, I'm staying with my folks and they're a little…changed since I went away."

"Changed? You mean physically, like surgically? Or changed like the pod people in that film? Because, you know, I've suspected for a few years now that my father might be a pod person." In his mind, Alex could picture the amusement lighting Damian's blue eyes, and for a second he really wanted to see his friend.

Alex laughed and warmth bloomed in him. "Actually, I wouldn't rule out the pod people theory. You know they both took early retirement? Well, Dad has taken up the drums—he looks like a demented octopus and sounds like he's rolling an oil drum full of bricks down a hill."

PUBLISHING

Sign up for our newsletter and find out about all our romance book releases, eBook sales and promotions, sneak peeks and FREE romance books!

About the Author

Ann Marie James is fluent in two languages, English and sarcasm. She believes that you will never learn anything new if you don't read as much as you can, and/or talk to every stranger you meet. She always looks for the best in people and to treat people the way she wants to be treated. Above all Ann Marie believes in love, whatever form it takes. Relationships are hard, love is the glue that keeps it together.

Ann Marie loves to hear from readers. You can find her contact information, website details and author profile page at https://www.pride-publishing.com

www.ingramcontent.com/pod-product-compliance
Lightning Source LLC
Chambersburg PA
CBHW030136180626
46812CB00002B/717